# The Great Cat Nap

## A.M. Bostwick

*Never Forget*
Cousins Louise
Van Oosterhout WX
Son Allen's, daughter,
Abigail Bostwick,
Author

121136

Amy Bostwick

Published by Cornerstone Press
Department of English | University of Wisconsin- Stevens Point
2100 Main St. Stevens Point, WI 54481-3897
(715)346-4342

Direct comments to cornerstone@uwsp.edu
Visit our website at www.uwsp.edu/english/cornerstone
Copyright © Abigail Bostwick 2013
*All right reserved.*

Library of Congress Control Number:  2013954887

ISBN: 978-0-9846739-2-6

Cover art designed and created by Rick Harris.

Printing, collating, and binding made possible by the generous contri-
butions of:
Worzalla Publishing
3535 Jefferson Street
Stevens Point, WI 54481-0307

# Acknowledgements

To all the readers who will join Ace on his adventure in the pages of this book, thank you.

To my family, especially my mom, Anne, and dad, Allen, who taught me to love books. For my sister, Alison, who loved my writing. And for Aunt Mary, who always sent me books.

Appreciation to my friends and fellow writers - here's to you, Nicci, Anna, Jenny and Sandra.

Thank you to the staff at Cornerstone, a wonderful team to work with. To Alice, my agent, for the million things she does.

Big thanks to the teachers in my life who put up with me and encouraged me to write as a teenager - Mr. Bob Colclasure,
Mrs. Kathy Wegner, Mrs. Jean English and Mrs. Mary Jo Wojtusik.

Mary Abigail, I'll never forget the first time you read to me. I am so proud of you.

A special nod to Lola, who is always at my feet when I write, and Boots, who prefers my lap.

Last, thanks especially to Wayne. You are my happily ever after.

To my friends and family,
including the ones with four legs.

# PROLOGUE

## THREE MONTHS AGO, JULY

Her striking beauty stared up at me from the front page of the Monday edition of *The Daily Reporter*. Even from the black-and-white mug shot published on recycled newsprint, it was evident pain-soaked tears were streaming from her bloodshot, baby blue eyes.

Yeah, being accused of first-degree, cold-blooded murder could do that to a pretty girl's face.

Name's Ace, and I'm a reporter.

I'm also a cat.

I didn't have time to think about the newspaper hitting stands and driveways tomorrow morning shattering the community's view of lovely socialite Miss Claire Emerson. Nor did I have time to crash for a Sunday evening nap after a hectic deadline; someone was tapping on the front door.

Padding a few steps, I peered through the extra large mail slot, bringing in a waft of steaming July humidity. I did a double-take. A stunning white Persian wearing nothing but an anxious expression was trying to get my attention.

She got it.

Straightening my whiskers, I held open the door to let her in. She gracefully leapt through and landed at my side in a huff. We were the only ones in the dark office.

"Is this how you welcome guests? Like newspapers being tossed onto dirty driveways?" she demanded. Her big, round eyes were blue, just like Claire Emerson's. I could smell the hot summer on her fur.

"Only if they're interrupting my nap. Name's Ace. What can I help you with?"

"I know who you are, *Ace*," she said haughtily. Her flawless profile stood out starkly against the outdated, paneled, ugly walls of the newspaper office. "Why do you think I came all the way downtown in this filth? This traffic? This heat?" She paused to shake her paws free of imaginary grime. The Persian eyed me up and down. "I need you to take a case."

"Detective work?" I questioned, half laughing.

"Yes, sir."

"Ma'am, I'm a reporter. I don't handle detective cases," I said, yawning. While I was intrigued by the stunning angel, it was obvious this was going the same place as when dogs chase their tails. Nowhere.

"But you *must* help me in my plight!" she demanded, pursing her mouth and scrunching her all too-pink nose.

I didn't flinch a whisker. "I can't get my paws dirty becoming a slanted reporter on the biggest story of the year. I'd be a cat marked for trouble."

"You must!" she squealed. I suddenly wished I had gone home with Max that night, my human companion and the newspaper's city editor. "*Pleeeease!*"

I sighed. Of all the rundown newspapers in all the cities, she had to walk into mine. "I won't do it," I replied.

The Persian opened her mouth to protest, but didn't

utter a word. Her dainty, furry face was suddenly over-
come by soft horror. She stared at the front page of tomorrow's paper. The headline blared "EMERSON ARREST-
ED, CHARGED WITH MURDER."

"Oh, you can't. You just can't!" she cried. "Are you
actually going to print this rubbish?"

I stood on the stack of Monday editions, examining her. She looked ready to crumple into kitty litter dust.
"Sorry, I didn't get your name?"

"My name is Angel," she said slowly, still staring
at the article. "Claire is my human companion. We live
together at The Heights. And you *have* to help me."

I took a step back. Or rather, four steps. Whoa, this
was a high-class cat. One who was in a lot of trouble, if
you asked me.

It'd be a great story.

But she wasn't here for an interview.

Angel looked into my eyes. "Oh, Ace, you just have
to help us."

Holy cats. With a pile of evidence ripe to convict
and nothing to go on to prove Claire's innocence, I wasn't
able to promise anything. I exhaled; I'd always been a
sucker for a pretty face.

"You can pay in tuna fish?"

"That's kind of steep," she hedged, sniffling.

"Well, a cat's gotta eat. And I'm on a reporter's
salary." I flicked my tail toward a bag of dry cat food by
the entryway. Kuddly Kitty Krunchies. Awful stuff.

"Okay, we have an agreement," Angel said, extend-
ing a paw.

I took it.

# 🐾 CHAPTER ONE 🐾

Outside the double pane window, leaves grew crispy and dry in the cold autumn wind. Their pigment was fading, transforming to crimson, copper, and gold. The wind shook the leaves loose and they fell below the barren branches. It was a beautiful way to die. In tune, a mourning dove cooed a sad song.

I stared absent-mindedly through the window at the county administrative office on a gray October morning. I was trying to stay awake during the Most Boring Public Property Committee Meeting of the Year. Possibly ever.

"I think we should rename the county fairgrounds Fair Fairgrounds," noted a male committee member wearing a flannel shirt and low-heeled boots which looked suspiciously feminine.

"Too hard to say," the committee chair, clad in a banana yellow polo shirt and ill-fitting brown polyester jacket, countered. "It should simply be Lakeville Fairgrounds."

"Oh, sure. Easy for you to say," chimed in the lone female committee member, her face glowing red. "Being from Lakeville and all. What about my constituents from

Branford? This county has *two* cities, you know!"

"I didn't mean to offend you or your constituents, Wilma," Mr. Ill-Fitting Jacket began to huff, turning a shade of cherry himself.

"How about Happy Fairgrounds?" interrupted another, running a hand through his thatch of balding hair. With that, they all burst into a single, droning conversation, each struggling to be heard over the other.

Right.

From my station under a plastic chair, I utilized my sharp teeth to untie Max's shoelaces. Max stirred and batted my paw away, mumbling at me to leave him alone, then looked around groggily, rubbed his blue eyes and mouthed a thank you for waking him.

Max was a good guy. He took me in as a kitten from the shelter during a cold, Wisconsin winter here in Lakeville. He was simply trying to write a story that day about funding shortages for homeless animals, but I gave him the big doe eyes. Max called me his "ace," or Assistant City Editor. The time spent at *The Daily Reporter* fostered my passion for journalism, and five years later I'm a short-haired, pure-bred reporter. I have green eyes, sleek black fur, and a black nose to match, but I'm too modest to tell you I'm a handsome fellow; when I bother to groom, that is.

The newspaper businesses could be fast-paced, ruthless, and never-ending.

Just not so much today.

Compiling information from hours-long county board gatherings such as these could be excruciating. Spinning a lackluster agenda item into a gripping article was most certainly *not* the exciting part of this job.

My mind back-tracked to this past July when my journalistic abilities had been put to the ultimate test. I've never been sweet-talked into using my reporter skills to play detective before *she* walked into my life.

Angel.

Despite the Persian's steadfast belief in Claire's innocence, I wasn't so sure. A few days into my investigation with the help of my best friend Sloan, however, gave me reason to believe in her. Much like writing an article for the newspaper, I gathered the facts, interviewed the players, and eventually put together the real story. Culminating on one dark and stormy night—just like the mystery novels say—the entire story broke when my good friends and I managed to nab the real killer. We even managed to alert police, bringing the killer to justice. Claire and Angel were happily reunited, and I ate tuna for a month.

Now, *that* was thrilling.

It was also dangerous. Reckless. I didn't like to think about that part so much. I hadn't planned to continue my detective moonlighting. I was, after all, just a reporter. The events of the summer both enthralled and frightened me. There were close calls and brushes with near-death, experiences most small-time reporters don't run into. It wasn't just my hide I was worried about; it was my friends. Risking our nine lives isn't something I should dip any whiskers into again.

"Is Fun, Food, and Farm Animals Fairgrounds still an option?" a committee member mumbled. "We have to cover this agenda item before we can move onto the next: enforcement of the speed bump in Parking Lot A."

I sighed.

## 🐾 CHAPTER TWO 🐾

Max and I entered the newspaper office later in the afternoon, escaping the biting wind as the door slammed behind us. Tied to the door were long forgotten Christmas bells, shaking in greeting. They were almost in season again.

"Well, Ace, I need some serious caffeine after that meeting," Max said to me as he headed towards the break room, running a hand through his tousled blonde hair.

Max lived at *The Daily Reporter*, well, practically lived there. When he wasn't here, he was at his little duplex a few blocks down. Like Max, I spent most of my time here at the paper. I only go home on occasion, but always stop by on holidays; better food. For the most part though, I prefer my solitude in the stacks of newspapers.

I entered Max's office, jumped on the desk and, with a flick of my paw, turned on the lamp. His office looked like every other harried newspaper editor's office: stacks of dusty papers, an array of awards hanging crooked on the wall, and a dead plant forgotten in the corner. I settled by the warm computer screen and listened to the wind howl outside.

*The Daily Reporter*, much like many other small, locally-owned newspapers across the nation, hammered out a daily read for a decent sized circulation of subscribers and newsstands. Seven days a week, staff put together the paper on a five-hour deadline to press. It was a stressful race against the clock day-in-and-day-out, but I liked the business. Newspapers are a dying breed, but without these watchdogs—and *watchcats—of* journalism, who would keep after the government? Report the bad news as well as the good? We did a fine job. *The Branford Examiner* was the only other newspaper publication in our county, honestly more of a disreputable tabloid. They boasted political headlines such as "GEORGE WASHINGTON REINCARNATED AS EGYPTIAN CAMEL," and breaking health news like "EATING DONUT HOLES LINKED TO RECURRING TOENAIL FUNGUS." I found their outlandish reporting style downright offensive to journalism as a whole.

Moving my tail off his keyboard, Max settled in at his desk, set down his steaming cup of coffee, and began to check email. I stood up, stretched, and thought about taking a snooze in my bed atop the filing cabinet as he deleted a host of junk mail, advertising ninja knives and miracle weight loss products. Just then, an incoming message marked "urgent" caught my attention. A poster flashed on his screen. An eye-catching, gray-blue cat stared back, limbs posed daintily as though promoting a top-notch cat food. Above her, red letters screamed "MISSING: PRIZE WINNING CAT."

"This is interesting," Max muttered, scrolling down the poster to read more. "Ruby the Russian, a Russian Blue five-time national cat show winner, has gone missing today, October 8. Reward offered for her safe return." A number followed, the area code indicating a Lakeville family.

I sat up and looked into the deep green, gold-fleck-ed eyes of the missing cat, a thin, pink collar with a silver tag around her neck. It was probably real silver. She was a famous type of cat breed often seen in cat shows; as a mixed Siamese myself, I rarely paid attention to those cat magazine tabloids that exploited rich and famous felines. There was something behind Ruby the Russian's eyes though, something haunting I couldn't quite put my paw upon.

Max hit "print" on the poster, sending it to the communal office printer. I ran to grab it, snagging it with my incisors and bringing it back to Max.

"Thanks pal. I'll give a call on this tomorrow," he said, setting it in his overflowing inbox. He'd probably need a search party to find it later.

I tried to settle into my bed for a cat nap, but I couldn't lose myself to dreams. *Cat nap. Cat-napping?* The blue-gray cat with evocative green eyes kept popping into my line of vision, demanding my attention. What if Ruby hadn't simply gone missing? What if she'd been taken against her will? What if she was in danger? What if she'd been *cat-napped*?

As the day came to a close, Max scooted out of his squeaky office chair and picked up a bag of Kuddly Kitty Krunchies.

"New and improved flavor, Ace," Max tried to entice me to my food dish. "Now with salmon-flavored x-bites."

I'd tried the x-bites. They tasted like artificial, salm-on-flavored, compacted bites of dust.

I rummaged in the bowl after Max and the remain-ing staff drifted out of the office for the night, carefully avoiding the x shapes. When all went quiet, and I'd had my fill, I switched the desk lamp back on. I turned to the telephone, pushed the speakerphone button and dialed my best friend, Sloan. I hoped his human companion, Mary, wasn't there to intercept the call. Sloan picked up on the first ring.

"Helllloooo?" he purred. Mary must be out. Sloan was a glossy Ragdoll mix with almond-shaped, gray eyes. Known for his cool attitude and tomcat lifestyle, Sloan was my longtime buddy.

"Sloan. Ace."

"Hey! Guess what? I've got a date with Misty tonight, the black and white longhair from 6B," Sloan said. Sloan lived in a downtown apartment building with Mary, kitty-corner from the newspaper office.

"That's grand," I replied absent-mindedly. "I'm wondering what you might know about a gray-blue Russian, though."

"Russian? I have a personal rule against dating Russians. Too demanding."

"Have you heard anything about a Ruby the Russian gone missing?" I asked.

"Huh," he pondered for a beat. "No, I haven't. But then again, I didn't see Lily today."

Lily was our chatty calico friend who lived at Anne's Coffee Cup, located downtown.

"I'm on the story," I relayed. "I have to wonder, has the show cat been cat-napped?"

My friend paused. "Are you investigating for an article or solving a mystery?"

My stomach clenched with apprehension. Sloan had been an integral part of my summer detective excursion. Since then, he'd been chomping at the bit for another crime to solve. But I wasn't ready. "Just the story, Sloan."

"Because you seem like you're *investigating*...."

"Reporting does call for a certain amount of *investigating*," I insisted, unwavering. Sloan sighed.

"Well, Lily's upstairs getting ready for bed at this hour. You know how early the coffee shop opens up. I suggest you go find some dogs living in the residential area," he offered. "You know what gossips dogs are."

"That I do," I replied.

\*\*\*

After hanging up with Sloan, I decided to take his advice. I was too agitated to go back to sleep, and the Kuddly Kitty Krunchies gave me a bit of an upset tummy. Exiting the extra large mail slot on the newspaper office front door, I inhaled deeply. The night was clear and cold, bright stars piercing the sky like diamonds scattered on black velvet. I exhaled, seeing my breath precipitate in front of me as I walked downtown, fur ruffled against the cool gusting air. Night came early this time of year and lingered until dawn.

Besides a few people dashing from cars to the front door of the downtown supper club, the sidewalk was mine. The community was still getting used to the change of the weather, blood not yet cooled to acclimate for the harsh winter Wisconsin unfailingly dished out every year. On both sides of me, quaint stone buildings rose, glass storefronts displaying their goods. Old-fashioned lamp posts dotted the sidewalk, casting soft, warm glows. People seemed to forget how historic, nostalgic, and unique these destinations could be. Unfortunately, once they started building and developing in East Lakeville, pulling in some big box stores and industries, downtown sort of died. Mom-and-pop businesses struggled to keep their doors open and the streets clean. The string of burglaries this past summer certainly hadn't helped.

Walking past the darkened windows of Anne's

Coffee Cup two blocks down, I came to a halt. The same poster from the email was hanging on the door. Ruby the Russian at her prize-winning best, missing and asking to be found. Keeping my steady pace towards the historical housing district, I saw many other posters stuck on the doors of businesses. The Russian's owners must have been out in full force today, handing out these posters and asking the public for help in finding their missing pet.

Or showpiece?

What was the life of a show cat like? A bustling, busy reporter, I was lucky to find the time to groom my ears and shoulders every morning. My claws were often long and sharp, and I was rarely given a bath. Max would be a glutton for punishment to give me *that* kind of treatment.

A cat who was on parade, on the other paw, was shampooed, groomed, clipped, glossed, exercised, and primped day after day after day. It sounded exhausting. Could a cat like that chase flies? Eat whatever he or she liked? Run down a mouse? Loll on the window for the afternoon? I wasn't sure, most of my friends were house cats.

Except for Angel of course. I remained friends with the high-class Persian after I brought her case to a close. Not only because she began to see a new light on cats who didn't wear diamond collars, but because my two other good friends now resided in her expensive building—Ally and Peter. Formerly homeless sister and brother felines at a rundown trailer park, Ally and Peter were key in cracking this summer's murder mystery. I adored the pair. I made a mental note to put Angel on my list of those I should interview about the case. I mean, story; she might know Ruby from the high-class pet salons.

A loud bark broke me out of my trance; I immediately and instinctively arched my back like the traditional Halloween cat. My mental musings carried me well into the residential district, and I wasn't paying proper attention. The homes here looked like they housed your typical two parent, 2.5 children families. Yards were neat and trim, sidewalks devoid of weeds.

"Ace, is that you?" a gruff voice asked.

"Farfel? Yes, it's me."

Farfel was a large Saint Bernard. When I say large, I mean roughly the size of a small car. Farfel's stature was intimidating and his near constant drool slightly nauseating, but his demeanor was friendly and kind. He often had the scoop on this neighborhood near downtown, and wasn't surprised to see me wander into his territory once every few months for the lowdown.

"It's cold out for a guy like you," Farfel said, coming to the gate of his fenced-in yard. Behind him, the Victorian house of his companions glowed warmly with lights and a television set. I could catch a waft of a late dinner cooking—Swiss steak and baked potatoes?

"I couldn't agree more," I said through the slats. "But I'm on official newspaper business."

"Oh, yeah?" Farfel's ears pricked up with interest, his eyes glistening.

"Have you heard anything about Ruby the Russian gone missing? A prize-winning cat, I understand."

"As a matter of fact, I have—" Farfel began.

We were interrupted by the insistent yapping, however, of Fifi and Fluffi, two white miniature poodles from the house next door. The two were just let out of their own home and they ran across the yard, squeezing through the gate into Farfel's enclosure. Farfel let out an audible sigh and looked towards the heavens as the two pink-sweatered pooches barreled toward us, competing for the lead.

"What is it? What is it? What is it?" cried Fifi, leaping up and down.

"Yeah, huh? Yeah, huh? Yeah, huh?" yipped Fluffi.

They then commenced yipping in ear-splitting unison.

"SHUT IT!" Farfel let out one, deep growl-bark, and the yapping ceased.

"You don't have to yell," Fifi snapped.

"No bones, Farfel," Fluffi agreed.

"We were having a conversation..." Farfel began saying, exasperated.

"About what? What? What? *What*?" Fifi squeaked, jumping in place.

"ZIP IT!" Farfel barked again. "Do you want your companions to call you in before you've gotten the scoop?"

That shut them up.

The three dogs looked at me.

"I was just asking Farfel if he had heard anything about Ruby the Russian going missing."

The poodles exchanged glances, visibly let down the "scoop" involved a feline, not a canine. They'd much rather have heard the Collie down the street had gotten a cosmetic ear lift.

Farfel ignored them, nodding grimly.

"As I was saying—before being *interrupted*—I have," the great dog said, casting a dirty glance at the nosy poodles. "It was just a few hours ago when my companions arrived home, and there was a knock at the door. I, of course, barked like the devil was there. Pam answered, and I noticed the woman at the door looked frazzled and upset. Pam asked how she could help, and the woman gave her a flier about this Ruby the Russian you speak of. The lady said her beloved cat had gone missing today, and it wasn't like her to go anywhere because she's an inside cat. Pam took the flier and said she'd be sure to call if she saw Ruby or heard anything."

"Did this lady give Pam her name?" I asked.

"Yes. But I can't quite recall it. It was something like Melanie or Marissa."

"I see."

"Pam did ask an interesting question," Farfel offered.

My ears twitched. "What was that?"

"She asked the woman if Ruby had a microchip for tracking. Unfortunately, I guess Ruby just has the type of microchip that can be scanned at the vet or pound if she were found. It can't actually be tracked," Farfel explained.

"How unfortunate, those chips are rare and pricey. Do you know if the lady went door to door?"

"Yes! Yes! Yes!" quipped Fifi.

"Uh-huh! Uh-huh! Uh-huh!" competed Fluffi.

"She came to your house as well?" I asked the whining poodles.

Fifi jabbed Fluffi in the ribs before pushing her face in front of her sister's to command all of my attention.

"That's right. She came to our door just after Farfel's and gave the housecleaning staff a flier, too!" she cried.

Fluffi fought back and stuck her face in front of Fifi, nudging her aside.

"FIFI! FIFIFIFIFIFIFI! FLUFFI! FLUFFI-FLUFFIFLUFFI!" called a shrieking woman's voice.

"Gotta go!" they cried in tandem as they raced side by side, trying to beat each other through the gate and to their back door.

"Isn't that a shame," I mumbled.

"They give me a headache," Farfel agreed. He let

out a long breath. "Does that help you, Ace?"

"It does. I'm much obliged, Farfel."

"You know, normally I wouldn't give two dry dog biscuits what happens to a hoity-toity cat—no offense— but there was something in that woman's eyes today that made me feel sorry for her. Let me know if I can help you in any other way. The owner loves that cat something fierce."

"That's just why I'm out to find her, Farfel," I said, turning back into the night.

## 🐾 CHAPTER THREE 🐾

Inside the warm newspaper office, I clicked on Max's computer. I waited as it groaned to life, then entered an online phone number directory site. I navigated my way to the reverse look-up section. Working on a keyboard with claws and paws was not altogether easy, but I managed. I poked out each number as though each key was a rodent I wasn't quite sure was dead or just pulling my paw. Without too much fuss, I entered the entire phone number from Ruby's flier into the search box, maneuvered the electronic mouse, and clicked the command "Go."

There was one hit: Horace and Madeline McMahon, 2479 Arbor Vitae Lane, Lakeville. Farfel had been nearly right when he said Melanie or Marissa was her owner. I clicked on the "Map" option to better see their location. Their home was near the Wisconsin River, not far from The Heights where Angel resided. These homes, however, were more like estates. If my memory served correctly, houses along Arbor Vitae Lane were located on at least five-acre lots with lush gardens, carriage houses, pools, and guest quarters. One wouldn't find pink plastic flamingos stuck in their lawns. I suppose I shouldn't be surprised. Showing cats was a hobby for any level income, but the wealthier residents here in Lakeville were especially favorable of this craze.

Next, I performed an online search of Ruby the Russian. An overwhelming amount of hits popped up, many from cat shows around the Midwest. Ruby had taken first place at cat shows in Chicago, Madison, and Minneapolis. Images of Ruby showed her from demure and modest to playful and mischievous. I knew it was the mark of a great model to have so many convincing faces, but did Ruby enjoy life on the road?

A website dedicated solely to Ruby the Russian featured a complete profile with her owners. A photograph depicted the happy family. Smiling, the man and woman were dressed in suits and holding their Russian Blue in a loving embrace. Ruby, stared into the camera, eyes unreadable but they looked content and serene. The profile went on to say she was born to two state championship-winning cats and came from a long family line of winners. At four years old, she was already a three-time national champ in her category. She'd also won six local and state titles during her lustrous career. Ruby was even featured in national cat ad campaigns promoting pet shampoos and fancy cat food. I shook my head. I was over five years old and hadn't even won a journalism award yet. This cat was making tracks.

Ruby had been shown since she was just six months old, I read. Acknowledged for her thick, velvety coat in shades of blue-gray, the regal Ruby had all the classic features of the coveted Russian Blue breed. The tips of her fur were slightly brushed with silver, almost like a sprinkling of powdered sugar. Her eyes were a signature dark green with gold flecks. She was truly a beauty, and I could understand why the judges lined up to pin ribbons on her idealistic appearance.

I glanced at some of the prize categories. These cats won not only ribbons and prestige, but checks for hundreds, and sometimes thousands of dollars. Others, like Ruby, were offered photo spreads in national magazines or even television ads. For a feline like this, the offers likely poured in show after show.

I scribbled down Ruby's address with my dew claw before yawning and turning off the computer and desk light. I curled into a ball by the keyboard next to the still warm computer screen and questioned my motives. Was this just a story on my to-do list?

Or something more?

\*\*\*

When I woke the next morning, drooling on the letters S and D, sunlight was spilling through the window. There wasn't a cloud in the cornflower blue sky. It was setting up for a nice day, I knew I had best take advantage of the sunshine and venture to Arbor Vitae Lane. Weather could be a fickle lady in Wisconsin; shining one day and pouring rivers the next, or icing you out one minute then heating up the next.

I shoved aside a stack of papers on Max's desk. Neatness was not a strong suit of my fellow city editor. After unearthing and noshing on part of Max's discarded day-old, sugar-coated donut, I left it all behind and darted out the extra large front mail slot. I stretched and breathed in the autumn air, its crisp tang filling my lungs. Slowly, I walked down the street to Sloan's apartment. It was early, and I had my doubts he'd be awake at this hour after his romantic dinner date, but sure enough, there he was in the window, gazing out at the bustling downtown. I waved, and he grinned before disappearing. He came out around the side of the building and joined me alongside a crabapple tree still clinging to a few brown leaves and shriveled fruit. A robin, late in his winter departure, picked away at the remains.

"I didn't expect to see you this morning," I admitted.

"My date ended quickly last night. Whew. I don't know. She's a great cat and everything, but she wants to settle down. Have a few litters. I just don't think I'm ready for that kind of commitment."

Getting attached to any of Sloan's girlfriends was like getting attached to teenagers in a *Friday the 13th* movie. Within minutes, they're gone.

"You'd probably gain eight pounds and never touch your cat scratcher again," I joked.

"That's one of my fears," Sloan said with feeling. "I'm just too young for all this family talk. Anyway, tell me about you."

I lightly pulled my whiskers, clearing my thoughts. "I'm on a story. Going to check out Arbor Vitae Lane to continue looking into the unexplained disappearance of Ruby the Russian. Want to tag along?"

Sloan sportingly agreed, and we set off. Along the way, I filled him in on the brief details I knew from the flier, the Internet, and from my discussion with Farfel, Fifi, and Fluffi.

"Do you think Ruby was cat-napped then?" Sloan asked.

"That's what my instincts are telling me," I said. "Here we have a rich house cat with no reason to leave the house other than her next grooming appointment or show. She only would have left crated with her companions. Why would she run away?"

"Good point," replied Sloan. "But it's kind of a sinister notion, isn't it? Why would someone steal a cat?"

"I suspect Ruby is valuable. She is, after all, a *prize-winning* cat. Some of these larger cat shows garner thousands of dollars in prizes," I explained. Sloan lifted an eyebrow. "Plus, the option of ransom. Perhaps she was stolen, not for her reputation, but to blackmail the family themselves. It's the ideal motive."

"Now I follow. Is the family rich?"

"Judging by where they live, they must have a sizable checkbook. I'm hoping we find some other friendly animals living there when we arrive so we can get the full story. Ruby went off the grid yesterday. If she was indeed stolen, I would expect a ransom note sometime today."

It took just under an hour for Sloan and me to reach our destination at a leisurely pace. Turning down Arbor Vitae Lane, we heard birds chirping, a leaf blower running, and the Wisconsin River gushing past. Small cities like Lakeville were known for their community members—members like these who lived and breathed the simple life that came with intimately knowing your neighbors, trusting them as your friends, and lending a hand when they needed you. Certainly this neighborhood, and Lakeville as a whole, would step up to help the McMahons in their time of need. I had to believe there was more good in these small cities than bad.

"How are we going to do this, Ace?" asked Sloan, coming to a halt and breaking my thoughts. "We can't just stroll down the sidewalk and up the driveway of Ruby the Russian. Her owners are up in arms about her mysterious and possibly criminal disappearance. We'll be hauled off to the pound!"

For such a cool guy, Sloan sure could lose his poise in a hurry.

"Don't fret, Sloan. We'll stay hidden by sticking to the hedges until we get to the house. Then we'll take cover in the landscaping until we can find some animal with information, or until we can enter the house."

"*Enter the house?*" screeched Sloan, looking at me like just suggested we board the doomed Titanic. "Perhaps I should explain some of the finer points of the American justice system to you, Ace?"

"That won't be necessary."

"You didn't mention this B&E back on Main Street! I'm too handsome to be behind bars."

"Come on, Sloan," I grinned. "You agreed to come along. We're best buddies."

"I'm afraid that's just what a jury of our peers will think."

I ignored his panicked plea and took off under the guise of the abundant cedar bushes, well clipped and easy to run under nearly the entire way to McMahon's mailbox. Gold numbers told us we'd arrived at our destination of choice.

Ruby's house was an expansive two-story: cream with green shutters and peach trim. The front door was entirely stained glass, a screened porch encircled the south side of the home, and the perimeter of the house was still flush with evergreens and late blooming flowers. Hardy white Shasta daisies, blushing mums, and butter-yellow marigolds lined the paved sidewalk. An extra large garage sat beyond the long, winding driveway. The backyard was neatly clipped and somewhat resembled a golf course. Taking in the scene, I considered our options: We could dart across the grass and take cover under the shrubs near the front door, then walk around the house to look for a point of entry. We could scurry a bit further and see if the garage held any clues.

Or we could go home.

I didn't dare ask Sloan, still nervous about an

impending criminal charge and animal lock up. For a cat so excited to embark on another detective case, he was as nervous as a cat on a hot tin roof.

"Let's shoot for that large mum, the red one. We'll take cover there, then circle the house for clues," I told him. He nodded in reserved acceptance.

Looking both ways, assured the coast was clear, we streaked across the lawn and tumbled under the flowering mum. This close to the house, we could now hear the hum of a woman as she worked, sweeping the floor. I believed we were near the kitchen, as I could also hear—and smell—an egg and bacon breakfast frying on the stove. I glanced up and saw a screen was open three windows down, letting in the clean autumn air. If voices were inside, they'd carry outside to our eager ears. I nudged Sloan and pointed to the window.

"Let's try to listen under it," I suggested in a whisper. "We might get ourselves some answers."

"Or a lawsuit," he muttered, then, finding his resolve, said, "Okay, got it. Let's go."

Sitting under the window, we stared upward and waited. After about 10 minutes of clanking and clashing, a woman called, "Madeline? Breakfast is ready. Would you like it in the study?"

Madeline evidently did not want the meal in her study.

"I'll take it here. Is there coffee, Tess?"

"Of course. Sit, sit. Don't worry so much, dear. Ruby will come home."

I exchanged an excited look with Sloan.

"I didn't sleep a wink all night. This is just awful," the voice that was Madeline groaned.

"Don't pick at your food; eat it," the maid, apparently named Tess, encouraged warmly. Was the term "maid" out of date? Perhaps it should be domestic assistant or something.

"Ruby would never go off on her own like this. I've called all of the neighbors, been to nearly every home on the east side. Today I'm going to the west side," Madeline said. I had a feeling it wasn't the first time she'd gone over this statement.

"Is that wise, Madeline? I don't think Horace would—"

"I'm going," Madeline said resolutely. "I cannot just sit idly by and wait for a phone call."

There was a tense silence. I could envision Madeline pushing her eggs around on her plate, abused and uneaten.

"I didn't mean to snap at you, Tess," Madeline said. "I'm just so scared. I love Ruby so much. I've raised her since she was a kitten. She was a gift from my father, may he rest in peace. Why, I'd give anything to have her back with me right now. I'd never put her in another show again, if only—"

Sloan and I didn't hear the rest of Madeline's sentiments. They were interrupted by a low, deep growl.

"Paws up," it said. "Back up you two. Nice and slow. NOW."

I froze. Beside me, I sensed Sloan doing the same. We turned cautiously and found ourselves cowering below a massive German Shepherd with massacre in his eyes.

The hair on the German Shepherd's back stood on end, his tail shooting out like an arrow, and his green-yellow eyes burning into ours. He looked agile, well-muscled, and 100 percent alert. The tips of chrome spikes adorning his collar flashed in the sunlight.

"Follow me," he growled quietly out the side of his mouth, sharp canines gleaming.

I glanced at Sloan, and we warily followed the dog out of the brush before he turned and came behind us.

"Maybe he's a nice, friendly dog..." I whispered.

"Walk behind the garage. Easy does it. Move it, guys," the no-nonsense dog ordered, nudging us along like common criminals. "NOW."

"...except he's, you know, just the opposite," I finished lamely.

We didn't have the guts to consider making a run for it. This dog was 10 times our size, twice as fast, and 20 times as heavy. This was not good math. It was much too risky to provoke this guy, so we did exactly as we were told. Out of earshot from the house, Sloan and I stopped behind the garage near a well-tended vegetable garden. Would this be our final resting spot? I gulped. Tried to look cool. We turned and met the eyes of the giant dog.

"Look, I'm sorry to intrude. I'm Ace, a reporter, and this is my friend, Sloan—" I began in a shaky voice.

"We don't need any reporters here," the dog began in a low snarl, his haunches bent like he was about to spring; presumably to chase our no-good, trespassing furry butts off his property.

"It's Ruby I'm worried about. Ruby the Russian. She's missing, right? Maybe stolen? I want to help bring her back," I said.

Something in the eyes of the great shepherd changed at the sound of Ruby's name.

"Huh?"

"Ruby. I heard she's missing. I want to help," I added, knowing full well at that moment that my intentions went far beyond an article. I wanted to solve the case. I wanted Ruby to come home safely. No matter where the story took me.

The German Shepherd looked over his shoulder,

and then laid down to better look at our faces. All of the fight seemed to have gone out of him, replaced by simple curiosity.

"Ruby went missing yesterday. POOF. Just like that," the dog said, shaking his enormous head.

"Exactly what I heard," I said. "Something doesn't seem right. I apologize for entering your property uninvited. I thought it would help me put together some clues."

The dog nodded. "My name is Aero," he said after a beat. "I'm the McMahon watchdog. Though I'm also a housedog. Ruby is the only other animal here. We're good friends."

I heard a catch in the dog's voice. Despite his intimidating size and threatening appearance, this was an animal who cared about his companions and his cat. I relaxed slightly; Aero was plainly a sheep in wolf's clothing.

"Why do you want to help?" he asked me, suspicion in his voice.

"Ace here solved a serious crime a few months ago," Sloan piped up. Aero's eyes grew wide with interest. "A murder. It was a big deal. He tracked down the real killer and we helped bring him to justice. We worked with this cat, who belonged to the wrongly accused woman. In the end, it was all set right. You can trust Ace. You can trust *us*."

Aero looked at me. "That true?"

"Well, I, uh," I began haltingly.

"He's too modest to tell you what a great detective and reporter he is," Sloan interjected again, shamelessly selling me like a late night infomercial. "This is the guy you want on your side. If he can solve a murder, he can solve a cat-napping."

"What do you charge?" Aero asked me.

"I, geez. I hadn't even thought about..."

"Last time, a few cans of tuna, plus expenses," Sloan interrupted for a third time. I wished my sidekick came with a mute button.

"I can do tuna. You're hired."

I coughed. While finding Ruby was certainly part of my personal mission, I hadn't expected employment by a private party again. I sort of figured I'd work on my own clock this time. Less opportunity for anyone to get hurt again. But Sloan smiled, fiend that he was, and Aero looked so hopeful I couldn't possibly crush his spirit.

"You don't owe me anything unless I bring Ruby home," I said, ignoring the panic rising in my heart.

"Agreed. What now? What do you need to know?"

We all feel silent as we heard a garage door open, then slam. The entrance door rumbled open, and a shiny black sedan slowly made its way down the drive.

"Madeline, with Tess. Looking for Ruby," Aero said sadly. We watched as they disappeared down the street.

"Tell me about the day Ruby went missing," I asked.

"It was just like any other day," Aero said, looking off into the distance. "I was let outside for my first morning run and perimeter checks. All was well, so I entered back into the kitchen where breakfast was served. Ruby always eats on the counter above me in her crystal dish. We exchanged our usual morning banter before she went off for her first morning nap in the sunshine of the library. I went back outside for round two of perimeter checks and detailed smelling. This usually takes me awhile."

Aero inhaled sharply.

"I was at the back of the property with John the gardener when I felt like something just wasn't right," he said. "Normally, I finish up my second rounds by 11 a.m., well on time to catch the mailman. I frighten and bully him on a daily basis, to make sure he knows who's boss around here. But this feeling wouldn't go away, so I made my way back to the house around 10 a.m. and went inside. Mrs. McMahon had left early for a meeting at the ladies' society. Mr. McMahon leaves each morning before the sun is up, so he was long gone. It was just Tess inside, and Ruby. Only…I couldn't find Ruby."

"What do you mean?" I asked gently.

"Ruby always takes her morning nap in the library, like I said. She's there until I get back; then she comes back downstairs for a snack before she moves onto the front sun porch," he assured. "But Ruby wasn't on the sun porch like usual. And she wasn't snacking. Or in the library, sleeping late. Or in the kitchen. I searched the entire house. I even missed chasing the mailman that day, I was so frantic looking for her. He arrived early and left the porch with a package—usually I just love to chase him off our property with a few good growling snaps, but I was too despondent. All I could do was send him off from inside the house with a few snarling barks. Ruby was gone. Nothing was out of place, but she was nowhere. I sniffed the entire yard, trying to catch her scent outside, just in case. But I couldn't. She's not an outside cat, you know. I barked, but Tess didn't understand. It wasn't until Mrs. McMahon came home just after noon that I could communicate something was terribly wrong. Ruby was missing."

"Tell me, did you pick up any strange odors during your indoor checks?" I asked.

"No. All the usual suspects."

"Who are?"

Aero thought. "Myself, Ruby, Mr. and Mrs. McMahon, Mrs. McMahon's sister, and Tess."

"Does Mrs. McMahon's sister visit often?" I asked.

"At least weekly. Don't ask me why; the two don't get along terribly well."

Interesting. "Why not?" I inquired.

"I can't say for sure, but the sister, Ellin, also shows cats. Only, she never wins prizes. Maybe a second or third place, but nothing like Ruby's wins," Aero said. "Ellin is newly single, and might be selling her house. I think it has to do with money. The sisters often argue about who had more as a kid, who was liked more...I don't know. It all seems silly to me. I don't even know where any of my sisters or brothers are. They should be happy just to have each other."

"Okay, let me get this straight," I said. "The last one to see Ruby was you, when she was leaving to take her normal nap in the library, correct?"

Aero nodded confidently.

"Did you actually see her in the library?"

"No, I didn't. But she was headed in that direction when I went outside. Just about every day when I return inside, she's already done with her snack, waiting impatiently on the porch for me," Aero looked upward sadly. "I never thought I'd miss her snide remarks about me dogging around with my big, ugly nose to the ground."

"Is is possible Ellin could have been here that morning? That you may not have noticed her?"

"I don't think so," Aero said uncertainly. "I'd hear her car."

"What if she parked down the street and walked?"

Aero examined his paw. "I guess it's possible. Had I been distracted, say, by John's egg sandwich, yeah. I suppose someone could have walked up to the house while I was in the backyard."

I nodded. "Okay. Tell me about this mailman fellow."

Aero's ears pointed up. "I've got a handle on him. He knows who's superior."

"But what kind of a person would you say he is? Are you sure this was the same mailman as usual? Not, say, a substitute?" I pressed, curious.

"Person? Well, he doesn't hate me as much as I wish he did. Sure, he runs when I chase him, but it's like his heart really isn't into it." Aero paused and Sloan raised an eyebrow at me. "And no, he wasn't a substitute. It was Frank all right. I remember the lingering smell from his socks. Look, Ace. It wasn't him. He liked Ruby fine. He delivers her trophies and ribbons all the time, not to mention all the cat food and treats sent by the companies that want to hire her for their ad campaigns." Aero rolled his eyes.

I pondered. Aero was young, smart, sophisticated, and didn't miss a thing. If he said the mailman was the mailman, I knew he was right. The next question I hesitated to ask, but as a reporter I knew I had to.

"Aero, would Ruby have reason to go off on her own? Alone?"

The German Shepherd looked surprised but was not offended. "Believe me, Ace, I asked myself the same thing," he said. "There hasn't been a robbery. There hasn't been a single strange person at the house. What does it look like? Like she left. I know, but I would have smelled her if she left the property by herself. I'm sure of it. You have to trust me, Ace. Ruby wouldn't leave of her own accord."

I reached out and patted his large paw. "I believe you. Can you tell me why Ruby wouldn't leave by herself?"

"She loved it here, plain and simple. Look around,"

the dog said, gesturing to his surroundings. "This is a great home, with great companions. We love our day-to-day routine. Ruby never complained. Oh, sure, she could be moody as the day is long. But she's a cat, that's a cat thing, right?"

The circumstances reminded me of one of those crime television shows where a person was victimized at their own residence. Since the door showed no signs of forced entry, the authorities would speculate the victim knew the perpetrator. Right now, I felt Ruby knew her possible captor.

"Looking at the information you've told me, I'm inclined to suspect only a handful of people. Tell me if I'm right, Aero," I began. "The gardener. The maid. The jealous sister. And most far-fetched, Mr. or Mrs. McMahon."

"All ludicrous suggestions!" Aero scoffed.

"As an unbiased investigator, that's what I see. Now tell me why I'm wrong," I asked.

"Okay. John the gardener is only here once a week, maybe more in the summer. He was busy trimming trees for winter at the far back of the property. John never goes in the house. I saw him leave, carrying only his clippers and coffee cup. He couldn't have entered the house in that timeframe without me noticing him, no way no how, much less smuggle Ruby."

I considered that. A man who never entered the house wouldn't know the layout. He wouldn't know where to find Ruby.

"Tess Vatter, our housekeeper is elderly and kind," Aero went on. "She's been with this family for over 15 years. She'd never have reason to cat-nap Ruby, nor did she open the door for any strangers that day. Mr. and Mrs. McMahan would never, ever hurt Ruby! They weren't even home, and they couldn't and wouldn't arrange for an outsider. I would've smelled him. Ellin may be jealous and have a bit of a mean streak, but, but..."

My heart jumped. "Yes?"

"She wouldn't steal Ruby." He paused. "Would she?"

Aha! A glitch in the list of alleged innocent suspects.

"Where was Ellin during the time of Ruby's disappearance?" I asked. "Could she have dropped by?"

"I don't know for sure," Aero said.

"Does Ellin have any animals I might be able to talk to?" I asked. "Witnesses?"

Aero nodded. "Yes, she has three cats she takes to shows. They're sisters, Himalayans. They live just up the road from here."

"Himalayans; the cats that look like their faces were hit with a frying pan?" I asked.

"Yup."

"What are their names?"

"Uno, Dos, Tres."

"I see. Clever," I said, taking mental notes at a fast pace. "Would you mind if I did a routine walk-through your house? It won't take but fifteen minutes. I just need to sniff around, get a feel for the place."

Aero nodded. "Yeah, but you better hurry. Avoid Tess, and don't drop any hair. She would yell at me for shedding more than normal. Trust me, *she knows*." I motioned for Sloan to follow.

The McMahon house was immaculate. The entryway opened up into a hallway with a winding cherry stairway. Off to the sides, several doors lead to more immaculate rooms. The kitchen appeared at the end of the hall. I sniffed the air: Humans, Aero and something lighter... feline. Ruby.

"You go upstairs, I'll run the downstairs," I said to Sloan. "Stand guard, will you, Aero?"

"I'll be here at the front door," Aero said, taking his stance. "I don't know how long my people will be gone, so be quick."

The study was dry, Ruby must not have spent much time here. I padded down to the dining room, keeping my back and tail low, darting glances every which way. Midday sunshine slanted in through the floor-to-ceiling windows, the maples outside flickering like a campfire. I sniffed the rug; someone had dropped a chicken leg a few days ago. In the kitchen, I sneezed. Cleaning solution overpowered nearly anything useful, but the certain regular scents of two human companions, one dog, and one cat were still apparent. I assumed Tess was in the mix as well, but it was too difficult to tell. Peeking out the door, I scanned the hallway. Aero remained at his post. I darted down the hall to the living room as fast as I could.

"Is that necessary?" Aero called to me. "Why do cats run so fast for no apparent reason?"

I didn't answer, I was investigating. A patterned sofa sat plump with pillows and throw blankets with fringes I'd like to shred. A large dog bed sat under a windowsill, a cat tree tucked alongside it. I eyed the cat tree, saw a few jingle balls, and an expensive-looking silk catnip mouse. Wouldn't a cat take her silk mouse if she were leaving?

Off the living room I saw the sun porch. Carefully, I stepped inside. Oohhh, yes. A cat could get used to this. The sun sunk into my back, easing the muscles and relaxing my aching tendons. Slowly, I circled the sparse but tasteful furniture. It was apparent where Ruby spent most of her time—here on her bed on top of the bookshelf. Even the maid couldn't vacuum all the velvet gray hair from its fleece. I tried to imagine someone—Ellin, the gardener, the maid—handling Ruby and smuggling her out of there. It didn't fit.

"Ace!" I turned.

"Sloan! Did you find anything?"

Sloan shook his head and stepped onto the sun porch, his body tense and eyes alert. "Ooooo. Ahhhhh. Wow, this is nice!"

"Right. About the case?" I urged.

"Huh?" Sloan asked, stretching long in the sunshine's warmth.

"Upstairs?" I reminded him.

Aero let out a sudden little bark. We both jumped. "Madeline and Tess will probably be back here any time now. Let's get outside before we're busted," he shouted from the front door.

We obliged and left to meet up with Aero.

"Sorry, Ace. Nothing but the usual suspects and some nice comforters upstairs," Sloan said to me in the side yard. "The library had Ruby's scent all over, but nothing unusual."

"That's all right. At least we know." I turned to the massive dog. "Aero, you've been an immense help. Is there anything else you can tell me?"

Aero thought for a moment. "Just that I'm worried about Ruby. She's an experienced show cat, sure. She's seen a good part of the world, but she doesn't know the real world. She needs help. I can feel it."

"I don't think Ruby left on purpose, either. I believe she was stolen," I said with certainty. Ellin. Ruby would trust Ellin enough to go with her. It would explain the lack of new human scent, no signs of struggle. Was it her jealousy? Or did she want money? Humans always want more money. "On this basis, I would expect you and your companions to receive a ransom note in the next few days, if not today. Keep your ears perked up for anything unusual, anything at all. Let us know right away if there is. Anything to add, Sloan?"

"How can we reach you here?" he asked Aero.

"Give me your number, Ace. I'll give you any updates I hear around here, especially about this possible ransom note."

"If Max picks up, just dial again after dark," I instructed, reciting the numbers. "Leave a blank message if I'm not in. I'll ring back soon as I can."

"I appreciate this, you two." Aero paused. "It was about this time yesterday when she went missing."

I said nothing, lost in thought.

"Now, if you'll excuse me, it's time for the mailman to arrive," Aero observed, examining the sun's position in the sky. "I have to chase after him, barking and snapping and portraying a ferocious, vicious canine who'd like to eat his shorts."

"Of course. You've got your job, and we've got ours," I replied.

# 🐾 CHAPTER FOUR 🐾

One thing about the newspaper business is you never know where a story is going to take you. Each day is different; a new adventure, a fresh angle, an event you'd never expect. It keeps me on the tips of my furry toes, and maybe that's why I like it so much.

But this detective business? This was another breed of cat entirely. Sure, I knew the pressure of a tight deadline. I understood the frustrations of not being able to work out every detail of the story. It was nothing, however, compared to the thought of a lost and helpless cat. It was nothing compared to the risk someone could be hurt.

Still before the lunch hour and still in the neighborhood, Sloan and I decided to check out the home of Uno, Dos, and Tres. There was no time to waste.

Ellin's house was about half a mile down the road, smaller than her sister's yet still a sprawling estate with climbing grape vines covering the impressive brick structure. The leaves were turning from green to a deep purple, the foliage crisp and crumbly as they prepared to go dormant for the winter. Perfectly trimmed bushes and a manicured lawn reflected a gardener on staff here as well.

It didn't look like she needed more money. The house
was set back from the road up a winding, uphill driveway.
Strolling up it alongside the scenery was nice if you liked
to pant.

Catching our breath under a late-blooming pink
hydrangea bush, Sloan and I considered our next move.

"I wish Aero could have warned the three cats we
were coming," gasped Sloan.

"He's a busy watchdog; we could hardly ask him
to take out his calling card," I wheezed back. "Okay, let's
think for a minute."

"And breathe."

"If you were a show cat living at this mansion,
what would you be doing at 11 a.m.?"

"Rolling in catnip with a side of caviar."

I gave him the "get serious" eye.

"Okay, okay. I'd probably be on the sun porch like
the one Ruby has," Sloan said.

"Good thinking. Let's stick to the side of the house
and see if we can spot the cats in the window. If we don't
spy any humans, we'll knock on the door," I advised.

Sloan nodded in agreement and we began our slow
course around the expansive homestead. We were much
more cautious this time, still getting over the shock of
coming face-to-face with Aero. The next pooch might not
be so understanding.

Underneath the sun porch, Sloan and I listened
intently for signs of life. Hearing none, we slinked up the
steps and peered inside the screened-in porch via the full-
glass door. Wicker furniture with thickly padded cushions
lined the room. Morning sunbeams poured in, reflecting
off the glass dining table where I could imagine a Sunday
morning brunch taking place. Ferns hung from the ceiling in complementing wicker baskets. In the far corner, I

spotted a towering, carpeted cat tree. On three of the levels were three identical tortoiseshell Himalayan cats. Uno, Dos, Tres, I counted.

"What do we do?" Sloan asked quietly. The cats were obviously sleeping soundly.

"We interrupt them. This is official businesses," I said with uncertainty. Waking up a cat, much less three, is considered somewhat suicidal in many societies.

Oh, well.

Sitting on my back legs, I pawed at the door. No movement. I pounded on the door harder. No response. Sloan and I both rapped on the door. I think one of the cats flinched a whisker, but still, nada.

"Excuse me? Helllooo?" I finally yowled.

The cat on the top shelf turned to stare at me through the slits of her eyelids. Her yellow eyes were irritated and unwelcoming. Her squished face appeared especially mean, pinched with fatigue and annoyance.

"We do not feed strangers," she hissed.

At that, the other two cats stirred and looked at the cause of their morning nap disturbance. Their pancake-flat faces replicated the angry notion of the first. With all six eyes fixed upon us, I felt just dreadful.

"Ma'am? I mean miss? My name is Ace, I'm a reporter, and this is Sloan. We're on a story."

The lower two cats stood up, turned, and laid back down with their backs to us. The first cat didn't move, but didn't look any kinder than she had to begin with.

"We're investigating the mysterious circumstances surrounding your neighbor and relative, Ruby the Russian," I said nervously.

That loosened the cat's tongue.

"You don't say?" purred the top cat, leaping down. "Come on in, our person is out for another few hours."

The others stood up, yawned, and gazed upon us with a mixture of mild interest and utter disgust.

The first cat took a single, graceful dive to open the porch door. It swung open, and the cat gestured with a bushy paw for us to come inside.

"So kind of you, thank you, miss," I said with a nod. She finally smiled.

"I'm Uno. This is Dos, and Tres."

I tried to figure out which was Dos and which was Tres, and then I looked at Uno and tried to figure out how to tell them all apart but quickly got confused. The trio were nearly mirror images of one another.

"Can I get you something? Sparkling water, a dash of milk?" asked Uno.

"No, thank you. We don't want to take up too much of your time. We're sorry to disturb you," I said.

"Indeed, it's not our style to intrude," Sloan interjected, smiling a Cheshire cat grin at Tres. Or maybe Dos.

"You're here about Ruby? Please, come sit on the davenport," Uno offered.

I didn't know what the heck a davenport was, but Uno indicated for us to follow her onto a flower-patterned sofa. Dos and Tres leapt onto a nearby chair. I wondered if it had a fancy name as well.

"Yes, that's right," I began. "We just came from her house where we spoke with Aero. We're concerned Ruby may be not only be missing, but stolen. She could be in danger."

Uno nodded. Dos and Tres stretched out and groomed their fluffy tails. I looked at Sloan, hoping he wouldn't drool.

"It is a strange occurrence," Uno agreed.

"She's awfully temperamental, that one," Tres said suddenly.

"What do you mean?" I encouraged.

"You'd think she'd revel in all that fame," Dos said.

"But she doesn't," Tres finished. I got the distinct impression these two were sides of the same coin. Uno seemed to stand out. What was the cliché? Two's company, three's a crowd?

"Now, you two, don't go speaking for Ruby when she isn't here," scolded Uno. "Mr. Ace, is it? How are you working to find Ruby?"

"Right now, I'm collecting the facts. I'm a journalist," I explained. "I heard about Ruby from a flier delivered to our newspaper. Something about the circumstances worried me. Now Aero is supporting our endeavor to find her and bring her home. I thought you three might be able to add some pieces to the puzzle."

"Humph," huffed Dos. "If Ruby is missing, it's because she wanted..."

"...to go missing. Her and that designer pink collar. Humph. She had such an *appalling* attitude," completed Tres.

"What did I just say?" Uno reprimanded her sisters again.

"Uno, would you say Ruby liked the cat show circuit?" I asked.

Uno hesitated. Unlike her siblings, she seemed careful to protect Ruby's privacy. "Well, at first she did. We're just a bit younger than Ruby. When we came to live with Miss Ellin, we were just kittens, but we were put in the shows early. Ruby showed us the ropes, made us feel at home." Dos and Tres examined their nails and exchanged coy smiles with Sloan.

"But did she like it?" I asked a second time.

"Not so much in recent years," Uno admitted.

"And why wouldn't she? All those trophies, all

those ribbons..." Tres scoffed.

"...all those prizes and all that adoration. All the commercials and magazines. Oh, it makes perfect sense for her to hate it," mocked Dos. I guess these show cats weren't exactly tripping over their own trophies.

"Stop, don't be such sourpusses," Uno said to her sisters. Turning back to me, she continued, "If you're asking me, and I think you are, Ruby was simply ready for a quieter lifestyle. Cat shows aren't always easy. You have to maintain a certain weight, your hair must be the perfect length, your nose the ideal sheen, eyes shiny, paws and legs flawless, tail faultless, teeth textbook-white, claws unscathed, tongue unspoiled. Don't get me started on personality; if you aren't playful enough, humble enough, mean enough, you don't get the ribbon."

"That's cutthroat," I offered.

"Uno exaggerates!" Dos trilled.

"We loooove it!" Tres agreed.

Uno rolled her eyes.

"All I am saying is it's a tough world. These are not household cat shows. After four years of being shown in the big time, Ruby was tired. That's all."

"She never said that to me," Dos said.

"Or me," Tres chimed in.

I asked the million dollar question, "Uno, would tiring of cat shows cause Ruby to run away?"

"No," Uno said certainly. "Ruby loved her home. She'd never admit it, but she loves that brute of a canine, Aero. Her companions are lovely people, she adores them. It's why she kept up the circuit. Ruby didn't have the heart to disappoint them. She could have thrown a show at any time, you know. Scratched a judge, hissed at a spectator. But she never did."

"Thrown a show?!" cried Dos.

"Well, I never! That would be…" Tres exclaimed.

"…horrible! I never would dream of such a thing!" Dos marveled.

I thought back to this summer when I was working to clear the name of Claire Emerson. In reality, she'd been working at her love interest's sleazy dance club. But she'd kept up her professional job under her overly-successful father just to keep him happy. Where did it land her? In a heap of trouble.

"Here's another question," I said, pushing my deep thoughts aside. "As a prize-winning show cat, would someone have reason to cat-nap Ruby? Was she…valuable?"

Uno, Dos, and Tres exchanged looks.

"This is quite a yarn you're spinning, mister," jeered Dos. I let that one go.

"Sure, she's valuable," Uno began, also ignoring her sibling. "Any show cat is. Here in the Midwest, Ruby is one of the best."

"Ruby's owners are valuable, too, aren't they? Wouldn't it possibly make sense to blackmail them in return for the safe return of their cat?" I asked.

The three sisters looked appalled.

"Would a person do that?" breathed Uno, obviously shaken.

"I don't want to be stolen!" Dos and Tres shouted in unison.

"Dos, Tres, we're worried about Ruby here!" Uno commanded. "I'm the oldest, can you tell? First born in the litter."

"To answer your question, yes, a person would do that," I replied. "I read court and police reports nearly every day. I report on unspeakable crimes, unfathomable operations, and unbelievable human acts. We have to expect the worst case scenario here if we're going to help Ruby. The faster we act, the better chance we have of finding her."

Uno nodded solemnly. "What else can I tell you?" she questioned.

"Tell me about Ellin."

"Ellin?" Dos and Tres bristled.

"All a matter of routine business," purred Sloan.

"Uno?" I prodded.

"Ellin is nice. We adore her. It's too bad she works a great deal of hours."

"Where does she work?" I asked.

"She runs her own quilting shop, Cozy Quilting and Supplies, downtown," Uno said. "She hosts parties and teaches private lessons. It's time consuming, and her hours are irregular."

I knew the quilting shop. It was Lakeville's lightning rod of sewing and fabric supplies. It was also the only one.

"Where was Ellin the day Ruby disappeared, between the hours of 7 a.m. and 11 a.m.?" I asked.

"I believe she was at work," said Uno, suddenly hedging.

"She wasn't at home. Is that what you know for sure?" I asked.

"Ellin would not steal Ruby, Mr. Ace," Uno said quietly.

"How *dare* you?" Dos called, looking as though I had just suggested we dump a litter of helpless kittens in the ditch.

"That's an awful thing to insinuate!" Tres snapped.

"I am not trying to offend you ladies," I said quickly, looking to Sloan for support. "As a reporter, I have to ask the tough questions."

"You have bad manners," Dos interjected as though there were nothing worse I could possibly be contaminated with. I shrugged.

"We don't actually think Ellin took Ruby. It's simply routine for the private eye to cross off any and all suspects. It's cool," Sloan drawled in my meager defense. Dos settled down, but still eyed me with suspicion.

"You have a snarky attitude, too," Tres called to me.

"I've been told, but what can a cat do?" I muttered. "Uno, did you notice anything unusual about the day Ruby disappeared? Anyone strange in the neighborhood? Odd visitors? Different behaviors?"

Uno considered the question. "Ellin was upset when she came home around 4 p.m.," she told me. "Madeline had already contacted her and told her Ruby was missing. Around 4:30 p.m., they both walked through the house, calling for Ruby. Just in case, I guess. That was the first we heard of Ruby being gone. Aero came over around 8 p.m., sniffing around. He was so distraught. But that's all that was out of the ordinary, we didn't hear or see anything else."

"I see," I said. "Well, we'll let you ladies get back to your cat nap. I mean, your sleeping routine. I'll be in touch if there's anything else I need to know. Uno, could you call me at *The Daily Reporter* if you think of anything else or if anything strange happens?"

"I'll do that, Ace," she assured me.

Sloan stretched, highlighting his toned muscles under that shiny coat of his.

"See you gals later," he said with a wink.

Uno walked us to the door. Just about to descend the steps, I felt a paw on my shoulder. I turned.

"I hope you find her, Ace," whispered Uno, her flat

face filled with genuine concern.

# 🐾 CHAPTER FIVE 🐾

It was time for a late lunch when Sloan and I reached bustling downtown later that afternoon. Before leaving Arbor Vitae Lane, Sloan and I did a quick canvas of the neighborhood. On five-acre estates, the homes were sparse, and few witnesses were found. The gray two-story next door was vacant, no animals of any kind. The brownstone kitty-corner sounded with a rude parakeet. Finally we found a middle-aged Burmese willing to talk—albeit untrustingly through her window screen—at an expansive blue ranch, two houses down.

"See anything interesting yesterday? I doubted a useful answer to the question, as her window faced the wooded backyard. "Have you heard of a cat named Ruby the Russian?"

"Shhh!" she scolded. She wouldn't let us in, or tell us her name, her green eyes wide and blank. "I'm listening."

"Because a crime may have occurred here in the neighborhood…"

"Shhhh!" she hissed again, staring above.

Sloan and I exchanged glances and watched as the

Burmese leapt straight into the air and swiped at a fly.

"Missed him," she glowered. "No. I saw nothing. I don't know Ruby the Russian. Wouldn't know her if she hit me in the face. I only read hunting magazines. Now, *if you don't mind*, I have hunting to do."

"What about your mailman?" I insisted. "Shoddy or an all right guy?"

"What do I care about a mailman?" she replied. "He comes to the door five days per week. So what? Good *bye*."

So much for our canvassing.

Sloan and I headed back downtown and padded up to the back door of Anne's Coffee Cup where our dear friend Lily lived with her companion—you guessed it— Anne. They ran this downtown coffee shop/diner, always serving up a warm meal, hot gossip, and a darn good cup of milk with cream and sugar. The sassy calico was taking in some afternoon sunshine as she pawed through the pages of a careworn romance novel, the front cover depicting a swooning woman and a man who apparently couldn't locate his shirt atop a jagged rock at sea. Anne was busy inside with the lunch crowd.

"Ace! Sloan! Can I get you some lunch?" Lily offered, setting aside her book. Lily had a sharp tongue but a soft heart. Her lively yellow eyes gleamed. "How about beef with vegetables tenderly stewed in a cellophane bag?"

"A microwave dinner? Absolutely," I agreed.

"Sounds perfect, Lily," Sloan called as Lily dashed off, taking her place in the sun. "I'm so hungry I could eat a rat."

"That's vile, Sloan," I answered his joke, thinking of our sort-of friend Boris the Rat, who also had helped us crack this summer's mystery. Boris, of all the animals in the entire world, was not the kind of creature you think could lend a paw to you in any way. We maintained distant contacts, never admitting we were friends.

"What do you think, Ace? Is Ellin guilty?"

Ellin had access and perhaps a motive: Jealousy. Financial gain. Ruby would trust her; but I wasn't entirely sure. "It's too soon for us to make that judgment, Sloan, but we will check out her supposed work alibi this afternoon. So far, she's the most suspicious party we have. I hate to say it, but I hope that ransom call comes in soon. It may be our best lead."

Typically, a crime has a host of suspects. It's a reporter's—or detective's—job to run them all down. Right now I could only pinpoint one: Ellin. I couldn't see Ruby's companions being the thieves, though perhaps the maid had a motive. For that matter, what if the gardener had an underlying cat dander allergy and sly hands? My journalistic nose also told me to keep a slot open for Mr. X. The unknown suspect.

The back screen door bumped open, and Lily came through, balancing a small paper plate filled with our lunch.

"Eat up! I had Meaty Beast earlier," Lily said, serving us the goodies.

"You're the best, Lily," I said, mouth full of beef. Gosh, this was way better than Kuddly Kitty Krunchies.

After a few moments of silence and munching, Lily twitched and looked ready to burst.

"Alright, you two!" she said, irritated. "What are you up to? I know it's *something* sensational."

Lily loved gossip as much as she loved her corny romance books.

"Ruby the Russian," Sloan spilled the beans. Or maybe the beef, dripping down his chin.

"Ruby? Is that so?" Lily asked with interest. "Her

missing poster is on our front register and our front window. What a shame." She clucked her tongue.

"We're trying to find out not only where she is, but if she's been stolen," I added, knowing quite well it was no good keeping a secret from Lily.

"Stolen? Truly?" Lily meowed, wide-eyed. "She's a super famous show cat."

I pulled out a carrot dripping in beef juices.

"Yes. My journalistic tendencies tell me there's more to this story than a simple cat gone missing," I confessed. "The McMahon dog, Aero, has hired me to solve the mystery. Sloan is helping me."

"You boys and your mysteries," Lily drawled in mock shame. "But I must admit, you did a great job a few months ago. If anyone can bring Ruby home, it's you."

"What have you heard around the coffee shop about Ruby? Anything?" I asked, ignoring and feeling sheepish at Lily's compliment. I never learned to properly accept praise, and I was still nervous about diving back into detective work.

"Oh, people are talking about it, but only a bit when they see the poster, nothing useful," Lily said. "I see Ruby in the cat show magazines every so often. Gosh, she's so pretty. What I wouldn't give for a day at her groomer."

"I don't think it's everything it's cracked up to be," I said. "Don't you think it would be tough? Having to look perfect all the time?"

"Nope."

Despite Lily's unsympathetic attitude, I could tell she was thinking about it.

"Do you have any magazines around with articles about Ruby?" I questioned.

"Hmmm. Let me go look. Need some water?"

"Sure."

Lily disappeared for a few moments while Sloan and I licked our paws, faces, and whiskers clean after the satisfying lunch. Lily came back outside, this time pulling a magazine with her teeth and rolling a bottle of water with her paws. Like Anne, Lily knew how to multitask. The screen door bumped shut behind her. While Sloan and I wrestled the bottle open to get a drink, Lily slowly pawed through the pages of the glossy magazine featuring every chic cat breed I could imagine.

"Here she is!" Lily spun the magazine around so I could get a better look, Sloan peering over my shoulder.

"Wow," he breathed.

Wow indeed. A full two-page, color spread featured none other than Ruby the Russian of Lakeville, Wisconsin. Her perfect blue-gray hair sprinkled with silver was thick and glossy, her eyes clear and sparkling. The reporter had done a decent job explaining Ruby's many accomplishments and awards, as well as detailed tips on keeping a cat looking as good as her. It sure was something, seeing a feature like this on a local feline.

"Well, private eye? Now what?" questioned Sloan.

"Now, we hurry up and wait."

## 🐾 CHAPTER SIX 🐾

By the time I entered the newspaper office it was late afternoon, and the sun had disappeared to nap behind a few clouds. I was ready to do the same. Sloan had gone home, but not before I warned him about calling Dos and Tres for business reasons *only*. The last thing we needed was a cat turning disagreeable due to a bad date.

"I was wondering where you were, Ace," Max said, happily typing away at his computer. I knew he was almost done for the day and looking forward to some late season fishing on this unusually warm Wisconsin October day. He polished off a can of microwave cheesy macaroni, tossing the empty container in the trash. Being a busy journalist with odd hours, Max rarely ate anything he couldn't nuke in three minutes or less.

I leapt to my bed atop the filing cabinet and began to nest around for the perfect spot. My own microwave beef had my belly full and my eyelids heavy. While disappointed there was no news of a ransom note, I still felt confident one would arrive by the end of tonight.

I had been dozing for more than half an hour, softly lulled into sleep by the steady click-clack of computer keys when I was jarred awake by a knock at Max's office door.

"Max? There's a Madeline here who said you wanted to see her after we finished her ad," Nicole, a graphic designer, said. Max smiled and stood to shake the hand of the woman who entered. I opened my eyes. She was tall, leggy, and blonde. She'd be beautiful if not for the pinched lines of worry around her mouth and her watery eyes, red-rimmed and exhausted.

"Hello, Madeline. I'm Max," he introduced himself. "I'm sorry to hear about your missing cat, Ruby. Please, have a seat. This is my cat, Ace."

I sat up and trilled in acknowledgement, hoping she wouldn't notice my claws hadn't been trimmed lately and my whiskers were askew. Flaws aside, Madeline smiled at me.

"He's lovely; so black and shiny," she observed. I purred in recognition, embarrassed by her compliments.

"Ace was a stray. The office lets me bring him in when I'm at work, which is a lot. Good thing Ace doesn't seem to mind hanging out here at the newspaper," Max said. "I think he prefers it to my stuffy apartment!"

Madeline tried to smile at his joke, but it was lost somewhere along a thin, wan line.

"Excuse me a moment, please," Max said. Max darted into the break room, reappearing with two steaming Styrofoam cups of coffee. He offered one to Madeline, which she accepted.

"Don't worry, many people drink my coffee and go on to lead fairly normal lives," Max tried joking again. Sitting down, he took out his notebook and clicked his pen open. It hovered over the blank pages. "I'd like to help you find your cat. What can you tell me about her?"

Madeline sighed. "Ruby was a gift from my father.

She was just a kitten," she began. "My father showed cats as a hobby, and thought a Russian Blue would be just the right way to get my interest sparked. It did, and Ruby just loved the show circuits."

Ruby's companion smiled in memory. From her purse, she pulled a small photo album and handed it to Max to flip through as she spoke.

"It seemed like she belonged in the shows. Right away, as young as six months old, Ruby was winning ribbons and awards. Entire cat shows by the time she was nine months old. So docile and loving, she never minded the hectic pace; though she was always happy to come home and see the family dog, Aero, and spend time there."

"She's a real stunner," marveled Max. Viewing the photos from my perch, I had to agree. "What happened the day she disappeared?"

"It was a day like any other. My husband, Horace, went to work. I left for a ladies' society meeting, and Ruby was home with Aero, the housekeeper, and the gardener. I came home around noon, and Aero was terribly upset. Tess, our housekeeper, didn't know what had gotten into him. But I knew right away."

Max looked up expectantly.

"Ruby was gone," Madeline choked on a fresh sob. She paused a moment, then continued after Max handed her a tissue box. "Thank you. I looked everywhere. Aero had his nose to the ground, running all over the house and grounds. It was no use. Ruby wasn't there. I called all our neighbors, then went to houses throughout the neighborhood and beyond. My sister helped me search, but she was nowhere to be seen. Just gone."

"Now, I'm sure she is safe and sound somewhere," Max soothed as he jotted notes. "She obviously has a loving home she wants to get back to."

Aero's story fit perfectly with Madeline's, like turkey on top of chicken.

"I've distributed fliers all over the city to businesses and homes. Now I've taken out a full page ad in your newspaper. I'm trying to reach everyone so that if they come across her, they know where to return her," Madeline said, staring into her coffee as though it might tell her the answers she sought. "I checked the local animal shelters yesterday and today, a few times actually, and of course they know to call me if a cat with her description comes in."

"Forgive me for asking, Madeline, but would anyone steal Ruby?"

Indeed. My fellow city editor and I did think alike.

Madeline sniffed. "Oh, I just can't imagine anyone doing that to poor Ruby. Or to us. Everyone loves Ruby, sure, but I don't think anyone would *take* her," she said.

"Is she valuable? I don't know much about purebred fancy cats," Max laughed, jabbing a thumb over his shoulder in my direction. "He's a mixed breed and shy. If I ever tried to put him in a show, I think he'd claw my eyes out."

That's right, buddy.

"Well, sure. Russian Blues cost a bit. And I guess because she's won so many titles, someone might see her as a commodity. Some of those cat breeders are terrible people...cat mills and puppy mills. I can't stand the thought of it. I believe in adopting homeless animals, I truly do," Madeline explained. "Aero came to us as a puppy from a pound, after all."

Madeline took a breath. "You don't think someone would steal Ruby to *breed* her, do you? She's spayed after all. It's not as though she could have a litter."

"I didn't mean to frighten you," replied Max. "You

know us journalists, we always think the worst."

"I never showed her for fame or fortune. I only wanted Ruby to be happy," Madeline said, tucking the photos back inside her purse.

"Don't worry. I'll write up a story, and we'll try to call as much attention to her as we can to find her," Max promised.

Madeline nodded, but I could clearly see the thought of someone stealing Ruby lingered on her mind.

\*\*\*

Still no ransom calls. No ransom note. No ransom anything.

I was beginning to think my detective abilities were as sharp as the x-bites in Kuddly Kitty Krunchies.

I paced the empty newspaper office, inhaling the fresh scent of newly printed black and white. Madeline's ad would run the following day. Max's story would be posted online tonight and ready for the next print issue; he had forgone fishing to make sure of it. There was no doubt in my mind that soon everyone in the city would know Ruby the Russian was missing. The only question was, what would the captor ask to return her safely? Coming face-to-face with Ruby's companion today had instilled me with one notion: Ruby was deeply loved. I saw absolutely no reason for her to run away.

First on the agenda, there was still the not-quite-empty cheesy macaroni container calling my name. Pondering my stalled case as I licked it clean, I finished and pushed it aside. I then turned on the speakerphone, dialing Angel's number from memory.

"Hello?" Claire answered. "Um, hello? Hellloooo?" She hung up. I waited another beat.

The white Persian with a diamond collar came on the extension with a purr.

"Hellllooo?"

"Hello, beautiful. This is your old pal, Ace."

"Ace! How lovely to hear your voice. I was expecting a call from Claire's new love interest. I do like to listen in. What do I owe the pleasure, dear?"

I laid down by the phone. "I'm investigating a story concerning Ruby the Russian. Might you know her?"

"Ruby? Sure. She and I visit the same groomer and pet spa. I don't see her often, but we do run into one another on occasion. Why? What's wrong with her?"

I told her an abbreviated version of events.

"Oh, Ace! That's just terrible! Who would *do* such a thing?" she cried.

"Criminals, Angel, criminals. What can you tell me about Ruby?"

Angel paused. "Well, just that she's one of the nicest cats I know. She isn't stuck up or snobby or anything. With a coat like hers, she has the right to be—but she's not. Sweet as fresh cat grass, that one."

"When was the last time you saw her?"

"Ohhhhh, let's see now. I suppose it was last month at the spa. She was having a deep conditioning treatment, and I was having a blow out," Angel recited.

There was nothing in that for me. I pressed on. "Uh-huh. What kind of mood would you say Ruby was in?"

"Ruby was the same as any other day. Cheery and friendly. Always calm, never out of sorts or angry. For all the prodding, combing, and clipping they did to her before her shows, I can't say I would ever be as patient as Ruby."

"I see. Do you have any other spa friends who know Ruby? Anyone who might be able to lend a clue?" I tried.

"I don't understand, Ace. How could they help?

They wouldn't steal her."

"No, but I'm trying to establish Ruby's contacts. Anyone who might have had a motive to cat-nap her."

"I just shudder when you say cat-nap. It's so scary!" Angel said, aghast.

"Are you *sure* no contacts come to mind?" I tried again.

"Well, if I had to choose someone who might have some fishy motives, it would be Ellin."

My ears perked up, and I leaned closer to the speakerphone. "Ellin? Why do you say that?"

"She comes to the spa with her three cats sometimes when Ruby comes in. I don't like those three cats, two of them I dislike *for sure*—" Angel gossiped.

"Back to Ellin—"I began.

"They think they're so great, like their litter box doesn't stink—"

"Right. About Ellin—" I tried again.

"—I think Ruby's companion and Ellin are related."

"Sisters," I confirmed, glad her attention had returned.

"Well, that explains it. I knew they ran some of the cat show circuits together. You don't have to take my word for it, Ace, but something about the way Ellin looked at Ruby just wasn't nice."

"In what way, Angel?" I asked, clicking my claws against the faux grain of the desk.

The Persian thought for a moment, trying to find the exact right word.

"Contempt, Ace. Pure contempt. It's like she's mad at her. I don't see why. Her own three cats are lovely, even if they are a little snippy."

I considered that. "How does Ellin treat Uno, Dos,

and Tres?"

"The three cats? Oh, fine, I'd say. They are pampered quite well. Though I think they spend more time with the maid than with Ellin herself. They don't seem to mind. *I* would."

"From the little you know of Ellin, do you think she's capable of theft?"

"Of Ruby? Oh, goodness gracious, I just don't know. I hate to think anyone is capable of such a deed, much less a relative," she said.

"I see. Angel, you've been a great help. Let's catch up for lunch someday before the snow flies."

"I'd like that, Ace."

I exchanged goodbyes with Angel and shut off the speakerphone.

Online, I pulled up a search engine for public court records. I searched the gardener and groundskeeper, John Sweet. A seatbelt fine back in 2008; not exactly a hardened criminal. I tried the maid, Tess Vatter. Not a single hit.

I let out a huge sigh and looked at the clock. It was nearly 9 p.m, and still no ransom note. This troubled me more than a knot in a yarn ball. Furrowing my brow, I curled on Max's chair and outlined my plan for tomorrow: check on Ellin's alibi.

# 🐾 CHAPTER SEVEN 🐾

In the world of newspaper journalism, it's all about timing.

Deadline after deadline, a reporter must be on top of every breaking story, every interesting lead, and every move that will happen next. Otherwise, BAM! You miss that deadline, and someone scoops you faster than an automated litter box. It's not to say you can be a haphazard reporter, however. Meticulous steps are necessary, recreating the entire scene if necessary, and ultimately finding sources who will give you all you need to know. Then, finding the truth.

Armed with that knowledge, I knew I had to recreate the disappearance of Ruby the Russian with careful precision. I had to investigate each of my suspects with the utmost care and configure who exactly had the motive, time, and place to cat-nap the valuable cat. My witnesses had run dry. It was time to check on the alibi of Ellin, the suspicious and jealous sister of Ruby's companion, Madeline. Also, my only concrete suspect.

A cloudy fall day was slowly dawning, the sky beginning to glow an icy shade of orange. Sloan waited

for me at Lily's back door bright and early. Yawning, Lily
motioned for us to come inside for a cup of milk. It was 5
a.m., and the shop opened for customers in an hour. Anne
was busy out front brewing coffee, pulling chairs from
tables and setting up the menu next to the register for the
day.

"Here's some milk with extra cream and sugar,
boys," Lily said, stifling another yawn.

"You're the best, Lily," Sloan replied.

"What would we do without you?" I purred, lapping the sugary treat.

"Any news of a ransom yet, Ace?" she asked,
pleased at my praise.

I shook my head.

"What does it mean, Ace?" Sloan asked.

"Maybe the captor wants to make the family sweat
a bit more. You know, let them miss Ruby before he asks
for all the goods."

Sloan nodded.

"So you're checking on Ellin's alibi today?" Lily
questioned.

"That's right. Say, Lily, do you know any animals
nearby who might be able to verify it? I was planning to
visit Farfel again, but I'm not actually sure if he'll know
anything useful. He lives too far from downtown."

"Pfft. Farfel only knows rumors. Dogs are *such*
gossips," Lily said. "But if you wait until at least six,
Birdie might be able to tell you something. She's a longhair elderly cat who lives just above Ellin's Cozy Quilting
and Supplies. She's in Apartment 2A. Sometimes, I bring
her deliveries. She doesn't get out much at her age. Birdie
watches out her window all day and all night long. Never
goes out, n*othing* gets by her."

"Great lead, Lily. Thanks," I said, rueful that I'd

never met this alleged great source before.

She smiled proudly.

"Angel thinks Ellin had a real jealous streak when it came to Ruby," I told my friends. "She said Ellin looked at Ruby with nothing but contempt. That's a direct quote."

Lily looked worried, and Sloan's expression reflected the same.

***

Just before the downtown clock struck six times, Sloan and I followed the back alley in the direction of the quilting store. I knew most of the dogs and cats within the vicinity of downtown, but I never met Birdie. According to Lily, she enjoyed anti-hairball cat treats, catnip mice, and only ventured outside the confines of her apartment in a carrier for routine vet check-ups. We came to the steps leading to the back apartments—there were three—and looked at each other.

"Do you think it's safe to awaken an older cat at this hour?" asked Sloan. "It didn't go so great the last time we woke up a few cats."

"Sure. Older cats need less sleep, right?" I reasoned.

"Since when?"

"I'm just trying to make sense of why we got up so darn early."

Padding up the steps, we pushed open an entry door and were faced with two doors and a hallway. Apartment 2A was on the left. A recently-delivered copy of *The Daily Reporter* sat waiting outside the door, its fold still crisp. I pawed lightly on the door, then we waited. And waited. I pawed louder. Silence. I could have knit three potholders in the time we spent sitting there.

"Maybe she's not home," Sloan finally suggested.

"Where would an elderly cat go this early in the

morning?"

I was considering rescheduling this unannounced visit when the door knob jiggled a few times and popped open. On top of a hall table sat a plump calico cat with soft, graying eyes and a short, stubby tail. Her focus narrowed in on us and widened with interest.

"May I help you?" she asked loudly.

"Hello, ma'am. Name's Ace, and this is Sloan. Our mutual friend, Lily, said it would be okay to visit you this morning," I said.

"Speak up, boy. What about a space loan?"

Birdie's ears were angled towards us. She must be hard of hearing. I exchanged a look with Sloan.

"NAME'S ACE. THIS IS SLOAN. LILY SAID WE COULD TALK TO YOU."

"Oh, Lily! Yes, such a dear, she is. Come in, come in. You should have knocked," Birdie purred in a broken tone, hurdling down from the table, grabbing the newspaper with her teeth, and pulling it inside.

"Let me help you with that," I said, taking a corner and eyeing Max's byline on the front page, above-the-fold article regarding a recent city council vote. This article would incite the mayor—but like Max always said—if the government was happy with you, you weren't doing your job.

The apartment was decorated with stylish, modern pieces. If it were 1950, that is. Birdie's companion was also getting on in years. She had a near indecent amount of crotchet doilies, covering practically every imaginable surface. The place smelled of stale bread and peppermint tea.

"I like your writing, dear," Birdie said to me.

"I didn't know you knew me," I said, surprised.

"What? You have a flea? Because if you do…"

"I DIDN'T REALIZE YOU KNEW ME," I shouted, patting my chest in a poor attempt at sign language.

"Oh! Yes, yes, Ace. I know *everyone*. Especially the animals and their owners," she replied smugly. "Can I offer you an armchair to scratch? A drink from the water bowl? It's fresh this morning. I only drink my water fresh—"

"NO THANKS. I WAS HOPING YOU COULD HELP ME WITH A STORY I'M ON," I hollered.

"No need to yell, darling. What kind of story? Is it scandalous?" she asked, leaning in my face. Her breath was hot and smelled of mushy, wet senior cat food.

"Ruby the Russian, a prize-winning cat, has gone missing. It's possible she was cat-napped. I'm trying to establish an alibi for a possible suspect. This is all off the record, ma'am," I said. Beside me, Sloan nodded. "I never reveal a source."

Birdie squinted and said, "What about Russian spies gone swimming?"

I sighed. This was going to be a long conversation.

"RUBY THE RUSSIAN IS MISSING. I NEED TO CONFIRM AN ALIBI," I relayed at the top of my lungs.

"Ruby! Yes, that lovely feline. I heard about her disappearance *days* ago—" Birdie began.

"Yes, as did I," I tried to cut off what I felt was headed towards a long story.

"—I follow all the lovely cats in those fancy feline magazines and what with Ruby being local and all—"

"Yes, yes, so—" I began again.

"—in my day, I could have won a few blue ribbons myself, I have no doubt—"

"DO YOU KNOW ELLIN FROM DOWNSTAIRS?" Sloan interjected.

"—I wasn't always this large around the middle…" Birdie paused, mid-pat of her ample tummy, and looked at Sloan, her eyebrows crinkling. "Don't think I don't know about you and your many dates, young man."

Sloan's eyes widened in abashment.

"THE QUILT STORE OWNER, ELLIN. WAS SHE WORKING OCTOBER 8TH BETWEEN 7 AND 11 A.M.?" I shouted, coming back to the matter at hand instead of Sloan's late night trysts.

"Is that the day Miss Ruby went astray?" Birdie asked me.

"Well, I never," Sloan huffed. I ignored his indignation.

"We feel Ruby may have been stolen," I ventured to the aging cat.

"I'm not stalling, dear. Now I asked you a question. Is that the day Ruby was misplaced?"

"YES. ELLIN IS HER COMPANION'S SISTER. WAS SHE HERE THAT MORNING?" I yelled.

Birdie may have been darn near deaf, but her mind and memory seemed intact. She thought for a moment, seeming to reel back her recollection of that fateful morning. Watching the comings and goings of downtown was this cat's life.

"No."

"NO? ARE YOU SURE?" My voice was starting to go hoarse.

"Sure as the feathers are yellow on a goldfinch in summer," Birdie said. "I awaken every day at 5 a.m. and sit on my cat perch to watch the people leave their apartments for work, and others who arrive for work downtown and to open up shop. October 8 was an unusual day for one reason, and one reason only."

Birdie paused dramatically.

"Tell me," I urged.

"What about a tree? I'm telling a story here, shush," Birdie scolded. "Ellin did not arrive at 7:45 as she usually does. No, siree. She did not arrive until 11:45. I remember because I had fallen asleep on my perch waiting, and her car door slammed, waking me up."

"I can't believe a car door would wake *her* up," Sloan whispered to me.

Birdie squinted at him but apparently had not heard his comment. I could tell she wanted to, but couldn't, reprimand him.

"Oh, I don't hear everything, but loud, sharp noises, I do. Ellin slammed that door that morning like she was mad at it," Birdie assured us, nodding. "Her hair was out of place, and she had a right mean scowl on her face. Something had gone amiss in her day. Now, I don't like to gossip like those canines down the way, but if I am to answer your question honestly, Ace, Ellin was not where she should have been that day."

The information troubled me. Ellin was late. Ellin was never late. Ellin had no alibi. Ellin had a bad morning October 8th. The only question now was the question reporters asked everyday: Why?

# 🐾 CHAPTER EIGHT 🐾

Sloan and I were not able to leave Birdie's apartment politely without first hearing of her early kitten-hood followed by a series of fortunate events that led her to live in Lakeville's finest Main Street apartment overlooking all of the city's best action. She then went on to introduce us to her prided hand-sewn catnip mouse collection provided by her owner each holiday. The threadbare and well-worn mice had names like Teensy, Weensy, Oopsie, and Poopsie. My mind was numb and reeling by the time we shut the door to Apartment 2A.

"That cat could talk the ear off a yak," Sloan sighed as we quickly slipped down the steps.

"I'D HAVE TO AGREE WITH YOU THERE, PAL," I screamed. "BUT AS DETECTIVES WE HAD TO REMAIN RESPECTFUL TO OUR SOURCE."

"Hey! You can speak at normal volume now, Ace," Sloan recoiled.

"Oh, sorry." I coughed. "That's hard to get used to."

"What do we know now, Ace? Ellin was late and disheveled. She's guilty."

"Not necessarily, Sloan. She just wasn't where she usually was," I countered. "Though it's not looking up for our prime suspect. We need more facts. It's time for a stakeout."

Sloan nodded. "Right. You want me to tail Ellin? I'll take the first shift and stake out the quilting store."

"Roger that, Sloan. I'll finish up at the office, check for a ransom note, and meet you around quitting time. If I have to trail Ellin home, I will."

"Whoa, you sure? Ellin's is a long way from home at dark."

I shook my head.

"Dark, Sloan, is the perfect place to hide someone. Ellin could lead me right to Ruby."

Sloan looked uncertain, but agreed.

\*\*\*

Ducking into *The Daily Reporter*, I found Max with the phone to his ear, humming along to the hold music. At the same time, he was packing up his work bag to head out for an interview.

"There's my assistant city editor," Max said, patting my head when I leapt on the desk. "I have to go cover an event at the school district. You better sit this one out. I won't be gone long."

Fine with me. Kids liked to pull my whiskers and try to make me wear their scarves and socks.

"3 p.m. Friday? Okay, I'll see you then," Max said into the phone, resetting it back into its cradle. He scribbled his appointment on a spare piece of paper, which he stuffed into his overflowing bag.

With one last pat, Max left the office. I pawed the door shut and began poking around the mess on my co-worker's desk. Among a stack of fresh faxes, I found several county committee agendas and one news release about an upcoming Thanksgiving parade. No ransom note. I hit the refresh button on the computer to bring up new email, but it contained no new clues. I scowled. I couldn't help but feel dejected. I was so certain there would be a letter to the McMahon's demanding an absurd amount of cash in exchange for the award-winning cat's release. I put on the speakerphone and dialed Aero's number. With any luck, he'd be nearby. The phone rang without answer.

I walked the newsroom and investigated the desks of other co-workers and graphic artists—they hated when I left filthy cat prints on their mouse pads—before returning to my office with empty paws. No ransom notes. Sighing, I jumped onto my filing cabinet and curled into a ball on my bed. Until this evening's stakeout, I could do nothing but sleep.

# 🐾 CHAPTER NINE 🐾

How did these professional sleuths do it, I wondered? I'd watched a few crime shows from Max's lap over the years. They understood the crime by first daylight, were swept into unbelievable passion with a lovely woman by midday, caught the villain by nightfall, and were home in time for dinner. Without a hair out of place.

I loved my job. When I wasn't gripped in the high pressure of the public eye, or obsessing about being a good reporter, I managed to enjoy myself.

I wasn't so sure about being a detective.

At least not when I awoke at a quarter to 5 p.m. on a frigid autumn evening. It was so cold, in fact, I could have sworn I saw outside my window the county board chair with his hands in his own pockets. Max was at his computer, a bulky and unflattering sweater around his shoulders, seemingly unperturbed about Ruby the Russian, unlike myself. It was day two of my investigation, and already I was second-guessing myself. Had I been right this summer? Should I just stick behind my byline and keep my nose out of affairs I had no qualifications for?

Munching down a mouthful of Kuddly Kitty

Krunchies while Max typed a few finishing touches on his school-themed feature article, I tried to find my resolve. Ruby was lost. Ruby needed finding. The humans were doing all they could and coming up with zip. It was my feline duty to help if I could, even if it meant using a hodgepodge of journalism skills I figured could apply to an alleged cat-napping. Nothing bad had to happen here.

The door to our office opened, and Randy the sports reporter dropped a copy of tomorrow's paper onto the desk in front of Max.

"Your story about the missing show cat made front page," Randy alerted Max. Max picked up the paper and glanced at the edition. Ruby's green eyes glowed, even on the dull, recycled newsprint.

"I hope they find her. Madeline sure was worried about this cat," Max mused. Maybe he was more concerned than I had been led to believe. "Though I think it's going to take more than fliers and ads."

Randy leaned on the doorframe. "You suppose someone took that cat? To like, show and make money or something?"

"I don't know, Randy. Something about the whole disappearance just seems shady to me, I guess. Maybe I write too many crime stories and spend too much time on court reports," Max replied.

Maybe I did, too. But it wasn't going to stop me from following my instincts. Not tonight. As I slipped out the office door, Max wondered out loud why I was out catting around so much lately, but I ignored him, as I often do. Off through the mail slot I went, into the starless night to find Sloan.

*** 

My best friend's fur was puffed and bristled against the frigid air when I found him hunkered down by the back door of Ellin's Cozy Quilting and Supplies.

"Brrrrrrr," he purred coldly. "I wanted to get some hot milk and cream from Lily's but was afraid to leave my station."

"Sorry, pal. Why don't you head on home and warm up while I take over? Has anything interesting happened?"

"No. I wish I could say it had. Ellin took out a bag of garbage and put it in the dumpster, a mourning dove sat on that wire and stared at me for much longer than was comfortable, and a vehicle that sounded more like a jet than a car drove by twice."

I nodded. "All part of the stake-out risks, I suppose."

"It was about as much fun as watching a cat shed," Sloan said.

"Right. I'll call you tomorrow with anything I find out tonight."

"You aren't going to stay with her all night, are you?" Sloan asked, standing and stretching.

"Only as long as her lights are on, and she's active."

"But how are you going to follow her home? You can't possibly keep up with her car."

"I haven't figured that out yet."

***

After Sloan took off for the comfort and heat of his home, I circled the quilt shop and looked inside from the front window. The store was empty, but there was a woman, closing up. Ellin. Folding a few reams of material, her pale face was pinched with fatigue and her dull blonde hair hung limp and lifeless like two tired curtains over her face. Ellin's frame was tall and thin, her clothing hung like oversized garments on too tiny hangers. She held little resemblance to her sister. As she counted down the till, dropping coins noisily into their proper slots, I relocated to the back of the building. Ellin's car was a small, blue, four-door sedan. If I could ride along one way, getting back wouldn't be such a burden. Trouble was I had no opposable thumbs to pick a lock and open the car door. A window was cracked despite the chilly weather, but not nearly wide enough to cram through my furry behind. Time for resourcefulness.

The alley stank of week-old garbage and decaying leaves. I shook an abandoned straw wrapper off my paw and paced alongside the car, thinking hard and fast. Ellin would be finished inside and back here any second. Taking a deep breath, I dove into an aluminum trash bin and rummaged. Yuck. Papers that should be recycled, an old banana peel, rotting flowers. All in all, about as useful as a watchdog distracted by a steak.

Panicked, I ducked for cover under the trash lid as the back door of the quilt shop opened and slammed shut. Ellin had left the building. Fumbling with her keys, she breathed a long sigh and wiped her forehead, heavily perspiring despite the chilly air. I needed her attention. Now. At the exact moment she opened the car door, I sprang from the garbage can, sending the cover flying and crashing to the pavement behind my intended victim. Ellin startled and gasped just as I hoped, spinning around and clasping her hand over her chest. A black streak in the night, I ran away from the sound, darted under the sedan, turned hard left, and shot into the open car door. Ellin evaluated the non-threatening trash lid, still clanking to the ground. Composing herself, she stepped away from the vehicle to retrieve the lid and replace it while I silently thanked my lucky stars a heavy car door hadn't slammed on my tail. I gained an additional diversion, allowing me time to hide in the back seat.

Attempting to blend in under the driver's chair, I held my breath as Ellin entered the car and revved it up. I could feel the motor running under my tense body while the car rolled down the alley towards Arbor Vitae Lane.

Country western tunes played softly on the radio. A man with a deep, twangy voice sang about his estranged wife, sick dog, and repossessed trailer home. Ellin hummed along quietly, oblivious to her furry backseat passenger. I relaxed just a little, taking in the car. The upholstery was clean and smelled like fake pine trees. Besides a non-threatening box of pink tissue, the car was devoid of any cat-stealing evidence, and I couldn't smell Ruby.

The drive took just over ten minutes, long enough for the country star to reclaim his wife and dog, though not his former residence on wheels. I heard tires pop over loose gravel. As the sedan slowed and pulled into the garage, I pondered; how was I going to exit the vehicle? I certainly hadn't brought along any extra trash can lids to aid in my transition as I had moments earlier. The garage light came on. I bit my nail. Now what?

Ellin moved the gear into park and cut the engine. I hoped she wouldn't look into her backseat, as the glaring garage light would do nothing to hide me. Thankfully she exited the car, shutting the door behind her with a sharp bang. I heard the side door to the garage open and the lights clicked off, then I heard Ellin shut the door to the garage.

Crud. She could be getting away, attending to a stowed away, abducted, and frightened Ruby.

I waited a few minutes to be sure no one would return before uncurling my body from its hiding spot and checking out the scene. This reporter was in uncharted territory. Looking out the car window, I saw the garage was largely empty, aside from a lonely push lawnmower and some racks stacked high with boxes marked "Christmas" and "Halloween." A hodgepodge of mismatched tools were scattered across an otherwise vacant tool bench. Certain I was alone in the garage, I inspected the front seat of car. Nothing useful to my semi-adept paws. The door handle was large and unlocked. I pawed it, but lacking the sufficient body weight to move the door, it seemed hopeless.

My body shivered, and my tummy rumbled. Kuddly Kitty Krunchies were never filling, but I had bigger problems. My tail was not tailing Ellin. I yanked on the door handle with reckless abandon. Again and again, I pulled and twisted, kicked, and jerked. I worked up a sweat in the fast cooling car when I heard it—a satisfying click as the door popped open slightly, and the dome light switched on. With a swift jump, I switched off the light to deflect any unwanted attention. I pushed at the door with my shoulders, first the left and then the right. The heavy door gave way, opening a crack just large enough for me to push my head through. Free at last, I turned and surveyed the sedan beast, feeling an immense sense of pride after conquering it. I felt bad about not being able to properly shut the door, but at least the lack of dome light would spare the battery.

Now, it was time to get to work. Sleuth work.

***

The doggie door on the garage was large enough for a canine the size of Aero; it made me wonder if Ellin once had dogs in addition to Uno, Dos, and Tres. Slipping into the overcast night, my breath created tiny clouds in front of me as I crouched behind bushes and looked towards the house. The kitchen light burned, and I moved closer to watch the show.

An elm tree stood stark against the night near the

front of the house. I scaled it in a few seconds, attempting to hide behind a few lingering brown leaves and peered inside. Inside, Ellin had just set out three cans of Meaty Beast for the Himalayans, their topographically-challenged faces chowing down on the feline equivalent to human fast food. I envied those cats.

Ellin turned away from the felines and tore open a cardboard container of a microwavable pot pie. After setting it to nuke for five minutes, she collapsed into a chair alongside a breakfast bar and rested her head in her hands. Was this the face of a guilty woman? A jealous sister? A vicious cat-napper? I couldn't tell. The microwave hummed while the cats finished their dinners, moving away from each other to clean their dirty paws, faces, and whiskers. Uno strolled towards Ellin, bumping her head into her closed hands in an attempt for a pet. Her owner awoke as if from a dream and softly stroked Uno's head. Though I couldn't hear her, I knew Uno was purring. Ellin's hands caressed the cat, and I had the distinct impression she was gaining as much love from this interaction as Uno. My resolve faltered slightly; was Uno right? Was Ellin *not* capable of maliciously abducting another cat?

The microwave beeped and Ellin took the steaming pie from the oven, dumping it unceremoniously onto a plate. As the pot pie steamed, Ellin stared tiredly at a magazine without bothering to flip through it. I had the feeling she was just going through the motions of a normal routine. A few minutes passed. I shifted in my spot, the cold air nipping at my ears. Raking through the pot pie with a fork, Ellin took a tentative bite. Uno watched her. Dos and Tres left the kitchen, presumably for a long autumn night's nap. Ellin couldn't have taken more than three bites before placing the mostly-uneaten pot pie uncovered into the fridge, snapping off the kitchen light, and leaving the room. I guess she wasn't hungry. Uno chased after her companion. I waited to see which room would alight next, and was dismayed to see it was the upstairs bedroom. Ellin was going to bed.

Not a stolen cat in sight.

## 🐾 CHAPTER TEN 🐾

I was full of cold, stale cream and disappointment.

"Well, it doesn't mean she didn't have Ruby stashed in the basement without food or water, Ace," Sloan advised the following morning at the back of the newspaper office. "That cat could be anywhere. Maybe she knew you were onto her, and she was trying to throw you off the trail."

Sloan's attempts at cheering me up were hollow. After Ellin and the three cats went to bed last night, I had quickly jogged back to the newspaper office, trying to avoid the coldest part of the night. All the while, my mind raced. Where was Ruby?

"Ellin has all the motive in the world to take that prize-winning cat," Sloan continued. "She needs money. She's envies her sister."

"Newsflash. The woman *likes* cats, Sloan," I countered, sugar spurring me on.

"Jealously is a fickle emotion in women, pal. You've got a lot to learn," my friend tried to joke.

"Let's just pretend for a moment our initial hunch is right," I began. "Ellin stole Ruby for personal gain and revenge on her own sister. What if she already pawned off Ruby? To say, an animal dealer or a smuggler. That would explain why neither of us spotted Ellin taking care of a mystery animal yesterday. If Ruby's already gone…Sloan, how are we going to find her?"

"Still no ransom note, then?" Sloan asked, knowing the answer.

I shook my head glumly. Silence fell between us as we wondered exactly what we'd gotten our paws into this time. Minutes passed when a soft growl startled us from our quiet thoughts.

"Who's there?" Sloan hissed, his back arched, silky gray fur prickled high.

"It's me, stay cool," a familiar voice replied. Aero came from around the corner, his large and demanding presence filling the space between us in no time. Aero looked as dejected as I felt. He was toting a plain brown bag, dropping it at my feet.

"Any news?" he asked, trying to hide the hopefulness in his voice.

Sloan and I exchanged looks.

"We've been working hard on leads, but I'm afraid we haven't located Ruby yet," I admitted.

The German Shepherd's face fell. He composed himself, nodded and plopped down next to us.

"I take it you haven't seen a ransom note?" I asked the downtrodden dog.

He shook his great head. "I can't figure it out. She's just gone. *Gone*," Aero said slowly.

"I know this looks grim, Aero, but trust me when I say Sloan and I are not out of ideas to solving this crime," I said, Sloan looking at me like I'd just sprouted a second tail. "I have some ideas about what might have happened. I think Ellin may have sold Ruby off the minute she stole her. Passed her off to a smuggler or another thief. That being the case, we need to look up some lowlifes who would buy stolen felines..."

"Stop, Ace," Aero said.

"...and I have plenty of friends in low places. Well, not *friend* friends, but you know, alley cats who know information they shouldn't. Rodents who are in places they shouldn't be. They can tell me who..."

"Ace, honestly," Aero interjected again. But it was like my tongue was on autopilot. It's the Siamese in me. Sometimes I just can't shut up.

"...who would have Ruby and where they might take her," I plowed on. "Not to mention your maid and gardener. I'll keep going on this; I'll miss County Board this afternoon, but that's okay. Really, I can't stand when they talk budgets on and on and on and on—"

"ACE!" Aero barked. "I want you off the case. Here are a few cans of tuna for your trouble, but we have no real suspects. Ellin? I don't think so. Our maid? Our gardener? They both have alibis; I overheard the Mc-Mahons discussing them. Did you know that John the groundskeeper is severely allergic to cat dander? I didn't. It's why he never comes in the house."

This was news to me, and not encouraging news, either.

"I don't believe any of it," Aero continued. "I don't know how Ruby left, but she's gone. It doesn't make sense to stop your reporting to chase after a cat who doesn't want to be found."

"But, wait, what?" I stammered.

"It's obvious. Ruby must have left on her own accord," Aero said.

I looked at Sloan. He remained silent, clearly as confused as I was.

"No, no, Aero," I replied. "That's not the case. Sloan and I definitely think Ellin or someone else close to the family could be responsible in some way. This is only day three."

Sloan nodded in agreement. "He's right, Aero. This isn't over yet," Sloan said.

Aero stood up. "I can't keep doing this. Keep hoping she's coming home when she isn't. Do you know what it's like? Watching your companions in despair as they make call after call? Comb the neighborhood over and over? It's terrible. I couldn't even go after the mailman yesterday," he relayed.

Sloan and I gasped in shock.

"I was duped. We all were. Ruby took off because she was unhappy," Aero whispered. "I thought she loved us."

I didn't know what to say.

"We won't give up," Sloan offered.

"I know this is upsetting and while I can't imagine your loss, Aero, we can't give up now," I said, attempting to console him.

"Forget it," Aero snapped, moving away in a fast trot. He called over his shoulder, "She's gone. You'll never find a cat who wants to be gone."

I made a futile attempt to run after the German Shepherd but stopped at the end of the block as he became nothing but a fuzzy blur. Panting, Sloan appeared at my side.

"What now, Ace?"

"We keep looking," I answered without hesitation.

*** 

I didn't even reenter *The Daily Reporter* for a pastry and fresh cream. The case of Ruby the Russian was gnawing at me, especially since Aero had lost all hope. Sloan had to get back to his own apartment, indicating that his companion, Mary, had promised him a heaping bowl of fresh Meaty Beast upon his return. I thought it sounded fishy, but I couldn't deny the guy.

The morning traffic rush was slowing down as I headed towards The Heights. The air was calm and crisp, and I was thankful for the lack of precipitation as my long journey passed beneath my four feet. I was acting on a whim. This visit to Ally and Peter was, if I admitted it to myself, the last tactic I could think of in my quickly-falling-apart attempt at feline sleuthing. Unless Ally could tell me about something—or someone—who would be capable of stealing a cat right out of their home, I was as good as overripe sardines.

About four miles north of Arbor Vitae Lane along the Wisconsin River, 30 floors of luxury apartments and suites rose before me. Outside of Ally and Peter's stately building, ornamental shrubs were clipped neat and tidy, and the fall mums bloomed. I met Murphy, the always-on-duty white terrier guard watchdog, earlier this summer. Hunching behind a red mum bush, I surveyed inside the building. Through the Windex-clean floor length windows, there he was, sitting regal as can be by the front desk. Slinking to the automatically-opening doors, I jumped just enough to make them whoosh open, then darted behind a silver-colored trash bin that likely had never met a piece of trash in its life. My distorted reflection shone back at me uncertainly, but I obtained just the reaction I was hoping for. Murphy barked, running to investigate. Upon his hurried approach I hissed, "Pssssst!"

Murphy, ears alert, turned on a dime and met nose to nose with me.

"It's me, Murphy! Ace." I put my paws up as he cornered me.

"Geez Louise, Ace, what brings you by?" Murphy asked, letting his guard down, but just barely. "You surprised me."

"I need to get up to Ally and Peter's apartment. Can you help me?"

Murphy took a look inside the building then nodded. "Sure. Can you wait just another 10 minutes? Rodney, the day guard, will go into the break room for another cup of tea. I can sneak you on the elevator then."

"I owe you."

The terrier knew his humans. In nine minutes, Rodney stretched behind his desk, picked up his "I Love the Beach Boys" mug, and sauntered into the break room. Murphy ran to the door, signaled them to open, and ushered me inside. At the elevator, Murphy told me which button to push. I took a leap and hit three buttons in addition to the one I needed. At the ding, I watched Murphy disappear behind the sliding doors.

Ally and Peter lived on the fifth floor in a fine apartment owned by Lucy Shaw, formerly married to the very man who'd been arrested for murder earlier this summer, Willard Dinglehoff. Happier than ever free of him, she'd relocated to a smaller, sunnier apartment overlooking the river. Lucy adopted Ally and Peter through the twist of events I had set into motion.

I tapped my toes softly at the door, hoping Lucy was out. I hadn't thought about her in my rush to get to the apartment following Aero's hasty departure. The tiny rectangular mail slot squeaked open, and two blue eyes looked into my own. They suddenly widened.

"Ally! Ally! It's Ace! He's come to see us! ALLY!" Peter cried.

The door popped open, and I was bombarded by a ball of fur and kitten fluff. Peter rolled me over, purring and rubbing. It reminded me of his ruthless attacks the first time Sloan and I met him behind a trailer at The Orange Flamingo.

"Hey, Peter...gee whiz...yeah...it's good...to see you, too," I tried to spit out as he purred and rubbed. "How are you feeling?"

"Fine! Fine!" he cried. I would never stop feeling guilty about the injuries he sustained this summer. The injuries on *my* stakeout. *My* first detective case. Peter miraculously pulled through after a brutal blow to the head. Ally and Peter, willing participants, never once blamed me, but I couldn't get over it. It was why I had been so hesitant to take on another case. Another case like the one I was on at this exact moment. Guilt seeped through me.

"Now, Peter, let poor Ace inside," I heard Ally say from inside the apartment. Collecting myself, I tried to flatten my black fur that Peter had manipulated into spikes and snarls.

"Hi Ally. I hope you don't mind my dropping by like this," I said.

"Of course not. Come on in," she replied. "Peter! Let him through."

"Tell me, Ace, what do you think happened to the weasel?" Peter asked, walking backwards as we moved further inside.

"The weasel? You mean Willard Dinglehoff?" I asked, momentarily confused. Peter, still a boisterous and outgoing little kitten but quickly growing into a cat, believed in a variety of conspiracy theories when it came to fairy tales. This was mostly due to the copious amount of catnip his mother indulged in during pregnancy. His tiny face, though sweet as can be, held the constant look of a cat who ingested too much feline-Prozac. The head injury probably hadn't helped his delusions.

"No, no, no," Peter said, shaking his tiny head. "The *weasel*. Around the mulberry bush, where he was laid out for the last time."

"Peter, please stop with this," Ally told him.

"The monkey, he was up to no good. No good!" Peter assured me, excited.

I kept my mouth shut. I knew not to light a fire-cracker when I saw one.

"It's no theory! The monkey wasted the weasel!" He began to sing, "All around the mulberry bush, the monkey chased the weasel, and all around the mulberry bush...POP!" Ally and I jumped. "...goes the weasel!"

Unsure of what to do, I smiled.

"Peter. Must you?" Ally laughed quietly.

"I'm not sure, Peter. But I'm sure you'll figure it out," I finally said. He seemed satisfied with that.

Ally invited me onto the cushy sofa where sun-shine poured through the windows, heating the cushions nicely. The furniture was plush and white. I was suddenly self-conscious about my dark coat. You wouldn't want to have a hairball in here. Carefully, I sat down facing Ally's lovely blue eyes amid shimmering blonde fur. Peter nearly sat on top of me.

"I hope you're both doing well," I began.

Ally nodded. "You're on a case again, aren't you?"

"What?" I coughed. The cat was obviously out of the bag. "What makes you think that?"

"Oh, I still hear a bit of gossip or so. And I read your newspaper, of course. Your paw prints are all over this story. I didn't think you'd be able to keep yourself out of mischief when it came to this missing cat. Ruby, is that her name?"

"*Missing*?" Peter trilled. "Rumplestiltskin is notori-ous for stealing stuff. I bet he's behind it."

"I'm starting to wonder if I'm the detective/reporter here," I laughed. "I'm on the story. You're right, Ally. I don't believe Ruby went missing on her own accord. She was happy at home with the McMahons. As a prize-winning show cat though, Ruby is a valuable feline a thief could make money on. The perfect motive."

"You mean in the show ring? Wouldn't other people recognize her?" Ally questioned.

"With a few tweaks, maybe not. What I am inclined to believe at this point is the captor will eventually ask the family for ransom. They aren't overly wealthy, but they do have more money than most," I said.

"There hasn't been a ransom note yet, then, I take it?" asked Ally.

"No," I admitted. "I can't give this up, though. The house dog, Aero, hired me to find Ruby." I left out the part about being fired. "He feels Ruby was cat-napped, but he's already losing hope. I know these excursions can be dangerous, but I haven't given up yet."

Ally gave me a knowing look. Peter chewed on a nail.

"I didn't figure you would. Tell me then, detective, how do you think I can help you?" she asked.

"I know you're a long way from your days at The Orange Flamingo, but I thought you might remember some contacts. I need to talk to a cat on the inside. A cat who knows the animal thieves," I said in a quiet voice, hoping Peter was distracted. He chewed away.

"Oh, I know these thieves. They steal for money, profit. Taking perfectly happy animals from homes for trade, breeding, and sale. Absolute filth" Ally scowled. "They are not as few and far between as we'd like them. Peter, would you be so kind dear, as to get Ace some Tiger Treaties from the kitchen?"

"You bet!" Peter took off at break neck speed to please me, the house guest.

Ally leaned in. "Are you sure about this, Ace? There's no one else on your suspect list?"

"Just one, but she's unlikely. The jealous sister… maybe," I shook my head. "The maid and the gardener are already out. No one saw Ruby leaving alone, or with a stranger. My gut is telling me this was a calculated crime., one only a truly immoral human being could carry out, someone who perhaps even knew the family."

Ally let the information sink in slowly.

"Look, Ace, I'll give you a name, but you must realize this cat has dirty paws. Dreadfully dirty paws. Don't push him, don't ask for too much, and never second guess him. He's the only guy who will know if a crook did steal Ruby. He knows all the trades, inside and out."

"Okay," I agreed.

"*Never* ask him how he knows," she instructed.

"Okay," I said, nodding in encouragement. We had to speak quickly, Peter's delicate kitten ears would return at any moment. It was enough that Peter believed in corrupt crime in his fairy tale books.

"Rogue. His name is Rogue," Ally said quietly. "His lady's name is Diamond. You'll find him in the back alleys of Sixth and Penny Street."

Peter came bounding back into the room, a small bag of treats hanging from his mouth.

"I foubt da tweets, Affy," he mumbled through the package.

"Great, Peter. Now how about that new jingly ball you have in the bedroom?" Ally asked, trying to distract her younger brother.

"Oh! Ace, you wanna see my jingly ball?" he shrieked, dropping the bag. "I'll go get it! I have to get it out from under the dresser first!" Peter was a cat on fire as he ran off again to delight me.

"Oh, Ace," Ally said quietly, shaking her tail in displeasure. "Don't you remember what happened to the curious cat?"

I smiled.

"Don't worry your little head, Ally. I've got this. I've been a reporter for a long time, nothing will get me off this story," I said.

"You missed the pretty."

"Pardon?"

"My *pretty* little head," Ally explained, giving me a wry smile.

If I could blush, I would have. Peter raced back into the living room, a bell rattling the entire way. He dropped it at my feet, an offering not unlike a dead mouse.

"Look there. Now that's a fine jingly ball," I remarked. "Did you wrestle this from under the dresser all by yourself, Peter?"

"Oh, yeah," he said, puffing out his little chest with pride. "All the time. I keep trying to bust it open. I think there might be a camera in there. They watch me you know."

"They?"

"Yup. *They*," he said gravely.

I could tell Ally wanted to say something more to me, but Peter continued.

"Don't worry. I'm not putting all my stock in my theories," he said.

"That's good, Peter, that's really good," I said, standing.

"Yeah, I got a waffle shaped like Bob Barker. I'm gonna make thousands off it!" he squeaked. I moved towards the door. Ally smiled and hugged her brother, shushing him.

"You'resmushingme," he muttered into her fur.

"Ace, you will keep me updated, won't you?" Ally asked me as I turned for the door.

"Of course. I'll be seeing you real soon."

Peter wriggled himself from his sister's grasp and bounded into my side for another hug. Ally's worried face over his shoulder was the last thing I saw before I left The Heights for the newspaper office

# 🐾 CHAPTER ELEVEN 🐾

Inside the familiar confines of *The Daily Reporter*, I picked through a container of leftover takeout while Max typed away at his computer. He was hanging around late, catching up on old, non-time sensitive stories before heading off to the late afternoon County Board preliminary budget meeting. While I'd normally attend this nearly-always heated political display, I had other plans.

Plans involving a good source with a bad reputation.

I planned to hit the street just after dark. The night came earlier each evening in Wisconsin as fall slid into winter. I had a vague idea of where Rogue's hideout was, near Penny Street, south of downtown. A shadier side of town near The Orange Flamingo Trailer Park, Penny Street was a hodgepodge of run-down businesses, ramshackle houses and back alleys. It certainly wasn't a regular tourist stop on the local Chamber of Commerce "Welcome!" map.

Max put the finishing touches on his article before switching his computer off and gathering up his camera and notebook with a sigh. Skimming over the County

Board agenda, he sighed again as he stuffed it into his canvas work bag. He worked his plaid tie, hanging loose around his shoulders, back into a respectable knot at his neck. He tried to comb his messy blonde hair. I curled onto his office chair for warmth.

"This will be a long one, Ace. You're staying the night, I see? I expect I won't see you until I'm back in the morning," he muttered. Patting my head, Max shut out the light and left the office. On his still-warm swivel chair, I decided an hour or two of shut eye before the evening excursion wasn't such a bad idea.

I didn't dream.

When I awoke, the office was empty and quiet besides the humming of computers and the ticking of clocks. I stretched and headed for the front door mail slot, it was now or never.

I let my keen eyes adjust to the night. The lights in Sloan's apartment were non-existent. I pondered briefly about his and Mary's whereabouts before heading off for Penny Street to locate Rogue, the alleged felony on four paws.

The evening was cold and damp, matching my declining mood of the task at hand. My paws soaked up the street's water, leaving my pads stiff and chilly. I took in street signs as the neater neighborhood transitioned into the older, sketchier part of the city. I had no idea exactly where to find this Rogue character; an alley was a lot of space when you're talking about a single cat's territory. I could only hope I didn't surprise the guy into an unprovoked attack. As Ally indicated, he wasn't exactly the kind of guy you'd phone up if you needed an organ donation.

Rounding the corner onto Penny Street, I paused. A lonely hound dog barked somewhere in the far distance, but otherwise the street was silent. Somewhere, someone was burning leaves, the smell acrid and ashy. Across the street a few sallow yellow lights burned in the shabby homes, casting oddly-shaped lights onto the sidewalk lined with an occasional rusty vehicle.

Taking a few tentative steps, I focused on front porches and window ledges for signs of a cat who might be able to point me in the right direction. The block held no felines out for a breath of nippy fresh air, and I was forced to go back towards the few struggling business- es that looked like they were closed up for the night, or maybe were in the early stages of foreclosure. The brick buildings were crumbly at the seams, marred with fading graffiti.

I entered a long back alley that dead-ended at a proverbial, but in this case, literal, brick wall. The sides of the alley were the backs of the saddened businesses, each with an over-flowing dumpster and pile of assorted rub- bish. Many windows were knocked out, the glass shards grinning menacingly at me. I rounded a chain link fence and looked yonder. The best thing I could do was turn around, so I kept going.

A nearly full moon hung in the sky, lighting my path as I walked among the dismal buildings, looming like giants in the shadows. It was deathly quiet. Too qui- et. Just as I was about to check into what looked like an old dog kennel lined with plywood and shabby tarps, to my left I heard a trash can rattle. If I was expecting Oscar the Grouch, I would have realized I was a long way from Sesame Street. Out came a scruffy orange cat, missing the majority of his tail, but not because he was one of those fancy tailless breeds. Clearly, he had made rather poor character judgments in his lifetime.

"Whaddya want?" the junkyard cat growled as he leapt to my side.

"Easy there, fella," I said, taking a step back from his mouse-scented breath. His fur was patchy and coarse. This cat had seen wars.

Suddenly, I felt myself surrounded from behind. I peered over my shoulder, careful to keep my cool despite my flip-flopping stomach. Backs arched, three more alley cats growled as they approached. Their eyes flashed as they circled me. Instinctively the hair rose on my back, but I lowered my body to signal I wasn't the enemy.

"Hey, I'm no threat to you. I'm just looking for a guy. Maybe you know him. Rogue?" I ventured.

I hoped the name would spark some kind of retreat from the menacing tabbies and tailless junkyard cat, but it only ignited their distrust. Exchanging looks, one said to the other, "Did you hear that, Tiger? What about you, Bob? Trespasser here wants to see Rogue. That shouldn't be a problem, now should it?"

I had a sneaking feeling it would be.

"Whaddya think, Kit Kat?" the tailless cat questioned.

They all burst into loud, heinous laughter and circled my body. I kept a wary watch on them, completely unsure of my next move. I was definitely outnumbered. Ally was right, I overestimated my abilities this time.

"Pretty house cat wants to talk to the mangy outside cats, is that right?" the one called Tiger jeered.

"I'm not here to challenge you or to cause trouble. I need his help. You can understand, huh? Rogue is a smart guy, every cat knows that," I said.

"Of course he is!" spat Bob. "But that don't mean you can get to him."

"Who the heck are you, anyway?" demanded Tiger, sending a cloud of dandruff and fleas into the air as he shook his head.

"Name's Ace. Reporter. I'm on a story."

"That right? Well we don't like cats nosin' around here, do we, Kit Kat?"

The one named Kit Kat shook his shaggy black head, a sneer growing on his lips, revealing sharp, yellow fangs. He was missing an incisor, but I doubted that would dull his bite. The three cats circled closer to me, fraying my nerves.

"I see I've bothered you. Maybe I should just go then," I offered enthusiastically. They crept closer, eyes burning.

"Gentleman! Gentleman!" a new voice rang out, causing the cats to back off. I couldn't be sure, but I thought a slight look of fear crossed their eyes. "Is this how we treat visitors? Tsk, tsk, tsk. Let's be nice. Who do we have here?"

The cats parted, their heads bowed, as—to my surprise—a gleaming mink walked through the crowd and up to me. He was small, but walked on his back feet to appear a few inches taller. His eyes were beady and black.

"How do you do? Let me introduce myself. I'm Minx. And you are?" He let the question dangle in the air.

It wasn't often one saw a mink in the city. Minks are a rare breed, typically bred in captivity for their luxurious coats. A member of the weasel family, minks are not only known for their beauty, but also their haughty attitudes and foul stench. Minx, for example, reeked like a damp basement.

"Minx. Name's Ace. I was just telling your friends here that I'm a reporter. I'm on a story. I'm looking for Rogue, and I thought he might be able to help me."

"Ace, huh? Newspaper, yeah? Writer, eh?" Minx hissed, coming to all four legs and snaking around me, checking out my size and scent. "I've heard about you.

You should write fiction, you know, since that's what you're spouting off here tonight."

"Excuse me?" I said.

The three alley cats slunk into the background, clearly at the mercy of this Minx fellow. Minx, nonplussed, draped himself like a cheap suit over a nearby discarded soda can.

"Or maybe Diamond?" I tried.

"Lady Diamond?!" Minx exclaimed, shaken. He stomped towards me, his surly eyes level with my own. "Lady Diamond? No one, and I mean *no one* sees Lady Diamond without Rogue. You *really* aren't from around here, are you?"

Apparently not.

"I'm sorry; who did you say you were again?" I asked. This weasel was working my last nerve. He was toying with me. Weasels are notorious for being, well, weasels. While I was no doubt on the losing edge of this scenario, I needed to bring this conversation back around to the matter at hand. I had to establish that I wasn't some pushover lap cat.

"I'm Minx, Rogue's sidekick," Minx said as he sat back up on his legs, raising his trim body in the air. His chest puffed out with pride like a bag of popcorn microwaved on high. "I, along with many others, was stolen for my fur, but Rogue saved me. Rogue's rescue has earned him my eternal loyalty. I don't let just *anyone* see Rogue."

The savage mink eyed me up and down with annoyed displeasure. His pointy nose twitched.

"Rogue saved a weasel?" I questioned.

Minx stepped back, offended. "Who you callin' *weasel*? I'm only shirttail relation to the weasel family!"

Semantics.

"I understand," I answered to the smelly bodyguard, trying to appease him. "Hey. Look. I get it. You're good to your friend. Rouge has given you your life back, and you owe him a great debt."

"That's right, but I don't like the looks of you," he murmured, petting his soft tail. "And Rogue doesn't take unannounced visitors, anyway."

I pushed down the impulse to call him a liar, liar, pants on fire. Rogue was in the business of anarchy, thievery, and mischief. While he kept his friends close, he'd keep his enemies closer.

"All right. I'll get out of here. After you tell me one little thing," I said.

"What's that?" the weasel asked.

"Oh, you know, Minx. This little thing you're dancing around."

Minx gave me a questioning look.

"The *real story*," I demanded.

Minx's deep black eyes narrowed. "*What* did you say to me?"

"Rogue would have arrived by now. A strange cat shows up in his back alley, asking questions to his toughs, to his front man, some regarding his lady, and yet he doesn't show up to face me? No. Something is amiss here. Tell me."

What was wrong with me?! I needed a mouse trap for my tongue. Firing off insults to a character like this could leave me on a lifelong hit list.

To my shock, Minx backed off a centimeter. He looked at Bob, the tough tabbies, and his black backup, but they only returned blank expressions.

"What are you trying to poke your paws into, Mr. Hotshot Reporter, huh? What?" Minx demanded.

"A case not unlike your own. An animal, a cat, is stolen. I think Rogue may be able to help me find her.

Come on, Minx, you know what it's like. Locked up, alone, no future. Work with me. I'll make it worth your while."

Minx eyed me for what felt like 12 seasons of the Dr. Phil show.

"Come with me," he said finally, flicking his long tail to his backup to follow me in case I tried something funny.

Minx led me into a former dog kennel lined with plywood. Inside, several flashlights were lighting the corners. The cats had set up a variety of boxes that exited out the kennel and lined several yards of the alley. Covered in more plywood and a few mismatched tarps, the cats established a shelter of sorts. I had no idea how deep this shelter went, or if it entered into any of the resident derelict houses. Holey blankets covered several surfaces, and bags of cat food lined another wall. At Minx's offering, I took a seat across from him in the center of the kennel. He struck a match and lit a candle for warmth. I hoped he wouldn't burn the place down, it would go faster than a chocolate cake at a Weight Watchers meeting.

Reading my thoughts, Minx noted, "This is just the entrance. We live in an abandoned basement around here, but strangers don't go into The Pit."

"I see. It's nice, real nice. You guys have done quite a job here," I said. I meant it. The tabbies, who now took to lying down around the perimeter, nodded. The black cat, Kit Kat, remained standing, eyeing me with a furious curiosity.

"You don't actually know Rogue, do you?" Minx said as more of a statement than a question.

"I don't. A good friend referred me. I hear he's the best, that he can track any cat lost in the stolen circuit. I need his insight. I'm running out of time."

"A dear friend of yours taken, then?"

"Not exactly, but any cat unwillingly taken from a happy and healthy home is my business. I'm going to bring this cat home," I asserted.

"A hero, then, eh?" Minx chewed on a piece of stale bread. "James Bond with fur, sans the tux?"

"No. Just a reporter, trying to solve a crime."

"Look, Lady Diamond ain't going to see you without Rogue," he laughed. "And Rogue is, how shall we say? Indisposed."

I exchanged a look with Kit Kat. If I was not mistaken, he appeared a bit troubled. The small space smelled like moldy dish rags—it was Minx. I tried to breathe through my mouth and ignore the foul stench.

"I don't understand. Where's Rogue?" I cleared my throat nasally.

"You need Rogue to solve your little crime? I get it. I do. You need me to get you to Rogue? Sure, I'll tell you. But I need *your* help first."

I watched the weasel over the flickering orange flame.

"He's in hard lockup," he said in a deadpan, defeated tone.

My eyes widened.

"Yeah, that's right. The pound. The shelter. Not the no-kill one, either. And he doesn't have many days left before…you know. Keeeeeccchhhh." Minx made a slashing motion across his throat. "He's on death row."

I sat speechless for a moment. The cat with all the answers on missing and stolen cats was now missing himself. This was bad.

"How can I assist?" I asked, taken aback. I looked around at the rough-and-tumble group of cats. I was sure they was not his only crew. If they couldn't bust Rogue out, how could I?

"I know about you, newspaper cat," Minx hissed. "You were adopted from a shelter. Your pretty reporter friend bailed you out. Didn't he?"

"Max is an editor," I muttered.

"But you were on the inside!" Minx insisted.

I nodded. "Sure. You're forgetting something, though, Minx. I was about twenty ounces of fuzz at the time. I don't recall much."

Minx huffed in my face. "You must recall something!"

"Look, Minx. I don't know what you want from me. You're a weasel, for crying out loud, and you can't weasel the guy out?"

"Stop referring to me as a weasel, or this discussion is over *right now*!" Minx scolded.

I put my paws up like I was caught red-pawed. "My sincere apologies," I uttered.

Minx pouted, but went on, "We've tried everything for a week. Me and the boys." He rubbed the back of his neck nervously. "This is a pro-kill shelter five blocks down. Security is too thick. The hourglass is running low. Lady Diamond has entered utter despair."

I needed to find Ruby. That was my case. Getting this Rogue character off death row was not a problem I should add to my list right now; but looking at the tabbies, I imagined Rogue behind bars with a tray for a cat box, a stack of old newspapers for a bed. I pictured Lady Diamond without her companion. Lastly, I imagined his cohorts here without a leader. Something is to be said for the integrity of the underground alley cat system. The world didn't work without cats on the inside, even the down and dirty ones. I examined Minx's face. I questioned if this weasel was playing with me, luring me into some kind of dangerous situation, but his face was as honest as a dog's when the meat is out of reach. I believed him.

"All right, Minx. I'll help you, but this is going to go my way. You're going to follow me. That's the only way I'll do this," I asserted.

The cats sat up at attention, their ears and eyes alert. I had given them a glimmer of hope. Minx winced, but seemed used to the typical feline leader who acted like a real pain-in-the-haunches boss.

"You got it, Ace. Once Rogue is sprung from the pen, you can use his resources. He'll owe you. Then you gotta bust it outta this alley for good," Minx snarled, making one last jab at my obvious inability to blend into their crew.

"Fine. I have to put together a team. You need to put together a team. How late is the shelter open?" I queried.

"Until 7 p.m. on weekdays," Bob answered.

"Since we're low on time, we act tomorrow night. Same time. We'll meet here," I faced all of the cats as I dictated my orders.

"Wait—what do you mean, same time? We go while the shelter is open yet? You totally loco, cat?" Minx grunted, leaning close to the flame, his face half-in, half-out of the shadows.

"Yes. I mean, no," I retorted. "I mean, yes we go while the shelter is open, no I am not crazy. Trust me on this. Also, I need you to gather some items for me: A credit card, a paperclip, a long piece of string, three wood shims, and four iced jelly donuts."

"Jelly donuts? Some kind of glue, you mean?" Minx narrowed his eyes.

"No. I might get hungry."

# ❧ CHAPTER TWELVE ❧

Dashing back to the newspaper, my mind raced faster than my feet. What had I gotten myself into? There was, after all, no guarantee that Rogue would even be able to lead me to Ruby. According to Ally he was a tough character, the toughest cat on this side of the Western Hemisphere, or at least the west side of town. Would he surely scratch behind my ears if I scratched his? There was no promise this would pan out. I was acting purely on instinct and adrenaline, which wasn't always the most unbiased and analytical action for a reporter to do.

Maybe that's what detectives did.

At the office, I pushed through the mail slot and looked for signs that Sloan had stopped by for a visit. Nope, no fresh scents had been rubbed in the usual spot. I vaguely wondered why he'd been out of touch for so long, but dismissed it for a leftover sugar cookie and cold milk in the break room. I had to think fast; sure, I'd put together plans before in greater amounts of time that involved larger criminals. This, on the other hand, er, paw, was a different heist altogether.

Booting up Max's computer and logging online, images of debauchery danced in my head and I reeled back. Was I truly going to facilitate a break in, a robbery of a feline tagged for death? It wasn't exactly in my line of expertise; I knew less about burglary than I did about the upkeep of sea monkeys. There had to be a better method than a break-in. If a mink with all his resources couldn't bust into the joint, I wasn't going to either. No—what we needed was a diversion.

Searching for the shelter online, I located the small operation that Minx told me about, not far from his lair. I zoomed in on a photo; the building appeared to have a single, plate glass door in front with a standard deadbolt and key lock. That wouldn't pose a problem if the shelter was open.

I clicked on the "Adopt Me" section. At least 15 felines in distress looked back at me. Could any of them be Rogue? I had no idea. Looking past the faces that tugged at my heart and gnawed at my kitten memories, I examined their cages. No locks. This was good, I felt relief wash over me. It looked like each cage had a peg that pulled out of a mechanical locking system, easily operated from the outside but not from the inside, even for the adept delinquent paws of one Mister Rogue.

While the website did not provide a layout of the building itself, it was easy to imagine that a hall that led to the dog and cat rooms laid behind the front desk. Getting past that desk would be the first plan of attack. After that, we'd have to take the challenges as they came. If we checked into all of the windows before putting our plan into play, that might give us a better idea of anything that might stand in our way to freeing Rogue.

Now—what would constitute a diversion?

\*\*\*

I slept fitfully at the office that night, not truly falling into deep slumber until after 2 a.m. The Christmas bells on the door woke me, signifying the arrival of front office staff. Rousing from bed, I gave my fur a quick clean and checked out my food dish. The water was flat and sour, so I tipped it over on the floor to alert Max to better keep up with my aquatic hygiene standards. In the break room I found someone had baked a loaf of wheat bread and sliced it for consumption. I tore off a piece and ran away with under it under the fax machine table to devour it in peace. The graphic artists didn't like it when I snitched food, especially cupcakes.

Satisfied with a full tummy, I ran through the office for a quick check, assuring there was no news of a ransom note—there was none. Undeterred, I stretched and left the newspaper office through the front mail slot. It was a classic fall Wisconsin day, the air crisp and fresh. Thankfully it dawned sunny, I hoped that the blazing ball would heat up the air for today's deviant activities. I padded over to Sloan's side of the street and looked into his apartment windows. He wasn't sunning himself in the morning light, striking me as odd. Curling into my own patch of light, I camped out next to a bare-limbed tree and waited. I was ready to doze off amid the buzz of downtown morning traffic when Sloan appeared in the window. He gave a half-hearted wave, then raised a single paw to indicate he'd be with me in a moment.

When he appeared, I almost didn't recognize my best friend. He'd been *groomed.*

"Sloan, I, uh, well, this is, um…" I stammered.

"Don't say it. I know what I look like," he mumbled, his tail low.

I didn't say it.

"But, but, how did this happen?" I asked.

"I'd rather not talk about it."

"I think it would help," I urged.

Sloan took a deep sigh. "Remember how Mary bribed me home yesterday with Meaty Beast?"

"Yeah. Was it all a lie?"

"Oh, no. She had the stuff. As I was scarfing my second can down, she grabbed from behind and..." he took a deep breath as he recalled the painful memory, "Stuffed me into a cat carrier."

"No!"

"Believe it, my friend. Mouth full, claws retracted, I had no options to fight her. BANG! I was locked in and on my way to Miss Fluffy Foot's Pet Emporium," Sloan said with wide eyes.

"I don't understand. How *could* she?"

"It gets worse. After I was bathed, trimmed, clipped, powdered, and brushed...she...well, she took me to the vet."

"Say it isn't so!"

"That's right. I was primped and preened at the groomer, then manhandled by a vet and stabbed with two shots," Sloan bemoaned. "Something about my health and rabies and all that nonsense. Those vets live to watch you writhe in pain!"

I nodded in utter agreement.

"How are your nails?" I asked.

Sloan extracted his front claws, showing me how short they'd been clipped. "I've been ripping up the couch pretty bad, but only on the back side! I suppose I'm fortunate she didn't have them *removed*."

We shuddered in unison at the thought.

"You don't need to downplay your misery for me, Sloan. What do you say we go cheer you up at Lily's? Get a donut? Some cream perhaps?"

"No, no. I can't see Lily all puffy like this. I licked all night, but it's no use. All I can taste is Very Berry shampoo. This is borderline animal cruelty."

"I'm sorry," I murmured, patting his shoulder sympathetically.

"Enough about me. What's going on with the case?"

I filled Sloan in on the events of my evening traipse to the dark alley and my run-in with Rogue's posse. I ended with telling him about tonight's date to spring Rogue with his bodyguard mink.

"A mink? Are you kidding me? A *weasel*? A few months ago, we got tangled with a rat, now a *weasel*?" Sloan cried.

"Minks are only a member of the weasel family. Like cousins. I bet they don't even all have Thanksgiving together."

*"What?!"* Sloan screeched.

"Never mind. I've told the mink who's the boss; me. He plays it pushy, so I'm playing it pushy. I'm calling all the shots, Sloan. I believe he won't override the situation. It's our last best bet to get to the bottom of what happened to Ruby. We've got to do this."

Releasing a mammoth breath of air, Sloan nodded. "All right, all right. I've gotta go home and try to de-puff, though, if I'm going to get together with a bunch of toughs tonight."

I agreed and headed back to the office, noting for him to meet me outside at 5:15 p.m., fluffy or not.

"Try rolling in dirt!" I hollered to him.

As the afternoon wore on, working alongside Max as he typed up several deathly-boring County Board stories, I began to second guess myself. Should I have asked

Sloan to invite more backup cats? Was it a mistake to only have a handful of felines and one weasley-weasel at tonight's party?

My biggest concern trumped calling in more cats. The image was still fresh in my mind, that dark and stormy night when Peter was hurt. I didn't want to risk that again; I wouldn't. Alley cats like Rogue's gang understood the risks, as did Sloan and I. My trepidation at pulling in other recruits was too large to put anyone else in harm's way tonight. We didn't need anyone else to end up in lock-up.

A few of us would have to be enough.

# 🐾 CHAPTER THIRTEEN 🐾

I caught one more cat nap before the office staff began to drift towards the door, with tomorrow's paper put to bed. Everyone looked bug-eyed and haunted, the usual reaction after a hectic deadline. Even Max looked like he'd had more than his share of journalism for the day, having reeled out several government stories for the front and inside pages and web. My cat dishes were refilled with clean water (after a scolding for spilling it and causing Max to slip and "nearly break his neck"—he could be *so* dramatic) and a new heap of Kuddly Kitty Krunchies. I flicked the x-bites on the floor and ate the rest. Despite the atrocious flavor, I needed my energy. Rubbing my head, Max turned out his light and said I should come home that night.

If only he knew.

Scenarios of what could happen tonight played through my head like a bad horror flick. My diversion tactic could work like a charm, we could free Rogue, run out of the shelter, obtain some excellent information as to Ruby's whereabouts...and then...what? We'd hug and shake paws? Suddenly, my B-movie turned into an after-school special. It was all a highly unlikely scenario.

The truth of the situation was this was risky business.

We might not be able to distract anyone. we might not be able to get Rogue unlocked. We might not get Rogue to talk, even if we did unlock his cage. In fact, we could end up behind bars ourselves.

I couldn't think like that. I shook my head and went outside early to wait for Sloan. Rustling my fur against the air thick with autumn chill, I let my eyes adjust to the darkness. It fit my mood, and I steeled myself against anything that might go wrong in the next few hours. I wondered where Ruby was on this night. Did she miss her companions? Aero? It was time to bring her home.

It was time to act.

*** 

Sloan and I hurried toward Rogue's hideout where Minx and his posse had agreed to gather for us. My best friend had only slightly achieved what he had hoped— while severely less poufy, he still smelled like an orchard.

"You told that stinky weasel to collect tonight's tools, right?" Sloan asked.

"Yes. Just be thankful that he is unbearably smelly, Sloan. Maybe his stench will mask your fruity aroma."

Sloan made a face but didn't disagree. I think he was getting more used to these dangerous outings and building more confidence in our abilities as undercover crime-solvers of the night. Even so, that didn't make this excursion any safer.

We hung right at the shadowy alley, waltzing in like we owned the place. I kept my tail high, my ears alert, and my eyes wavered from one corner to the next in distrustful watchfulness. I wasn't about to let my guard down. Near the compound of the secret kennel/plywood/basement entrance, I made out the outline of five cats and the mink at the front of the herd. Minx's short arms were crossed in front of his chest, trying to stand tall. A brown paper lunch bag laid crumpled at his feet.

"Minx."

"Ace."

"Kit Kat, Tiger, Bob and..."I trialed off, unsure of the others' names.

"This is Sin, and that's Lobo and Onyx," Tiger relayed. Besides the original males, there sat a skinny male calico cat and gray long-male female with a wide rump, Onyx and Lobo, respectively. Sin was white as a ghost and lean, her eyes light green.

"Our claws are sharp and we're ready to go, Ace," Kit Kat rasped, the first words he'd ever said to me directly. The other five cats nodded in unison. "It's time to release Rogue."

"Yes, it is," I asserted. "You've got all I asked for?" They nodded. "Good. Let's go. Leave the donuts here."

***

I was surprised at the gang's eagerness to follow me. As a marauder of the night, Minx undulated ahead of us all, his lithe body taunt with unbridled anticipation. The energy of the night overshadowed any looming anxiety I had been feeling. It was now nearing quitting time for the pound but not so close that anyone might be thinking about locking the doors early. Few cars passed by this part of Lakeville in the evening, but we stuck to the shadows regardless, keeping wary eyes open for any signs of trouble. As it turned out, no one wanted to mess with five dangerous-looking felines, one black cat reporter, a freshly-groomed Ragdoll, and a shiny mink with an attitude problem.

Nearing the pound, we paused to regroup under an ailing cedar bush roughly the size of a yard barn. From behind a clump of decaying foliage, I took in the view of the animal shelter. The building was a small one-story with few windows, and two cement, decorative dogs flanked the sidewalk. A light shone out of the clear, plate-glass door that swung towards the inside. The parking lot was vacant, there were no visitors.

"All right, *detective*," Minx spat. "What's the gig? What're we gonna do here tonight that I haven't done before?"

You'd think the guy didn't even want me here. I replied, "One question, Minx. How did Rogue end up in lock up?"

The weasel hesitated. The five alley cats all pretended to be busy looking at their tails or the emerging stars.

"He was tryin' to bust out another inmate after closing hours," Minx answered in a flat tone.

I ruminated on his statement.

"Gutsy. Okay. How did he enter the building then?" I questioned.

"Walked right in after picking the lock. He knows a bulldog south of Penny Street that has the tools to work anything. He balanced on the door handle to jimmy the locks. The dog pulled open the door."

"Then what?"

"Isn't this something we should have thought about *before* we came down here tonight?" Sloan snapped, dread dripping from his voice.

I urged Minx to continue.

"The shelter wasn't so closed after all. Some staff were still behind, cleaning up the floors and trash cans. The bulldog ran like mad, the door slammed behind

Rogue and trapped him inside. Some brute snatched Rogue while he was off guard. BOOM. Tossed behind bars."

"And since you couldn't bust him out, and no one adopted him..." I began.

"...he's tagged to be gassed," Minx finished.

If I wasn't mistaken, I heard a catch in Minx's voice. I supposed besides following the tough cat, he also had affection for him not unlike the friendship I had with Sloan, who was growing more and more annoyed with me by the minute.

"I see. Thanks, Minx, now we know where Rogue went wrong. We aren't going to make that mistake to-night," I told the cats. They seemed agreeable, but Minx's gaze could cut steel wire.

"What a fine time to bring *this* up," he lashed out. "You indicated to me that you had a concrete plan that would work, Mr. Jelly Donut." He paused dramatically, then spat, "You lied to me."

"And it was entirely to my enjoyment," I snapped back. "And I do have a plan. No plan is concrete—look at what happened to Rogue, the mastermind. We have to stay flexible. Now start unpacking."

Minx narrowed his eyes, an unflattering scowl plas-tered on his face but he obeyed, pulling out the string first.

"Sloan, take the string and stick by my side. Minx, you take the wooden shims, they're important. Kit Kat, the paperclip. Tiger, the credit card. Bob, Onyx, Lobo, and Sin? You're all the diversion. This is crucial; tonight's plan can be summed up in one word: *Diversion*. We are going to *divert* all of the attention of any staff inside that building. We have power in numbers."

I took a breath and hoped my lesson plan didn't sound like Creative Vocabulary 101.

"Step one," I went on. "We need to stick together and check out all the windows of the place to pinpoint the exact location of Rogue's cage, as well as establish how many humans are inside. I need all eyes inside that building. Memorize the layout. Memorize everything you can. Once we've done that, you're going to follow my lead. Got it?"

Everyone meowed their assent, and we crept toward the side of the shelter, leaping up onto a well-placed dumpster to peer into a high rectangular, window. A low light glowed, illuminating rows of kennels. Bingo was his name-o; about a half dozen canines curled into balls atop threadbare beds on cold, concrete floors, the dogs spread between 12 separate cages, six on each side. I saw a cabinet missing one door that appeared to house towels and spare dog toys, some boxes of biscuits.

"Ladies, um, lady, and gentleman, we may need these dogs to bark. I mean bark like the devil, okay? Wait for the cue," I instructed.

Minx looked annoyed, but the cats all nodded. Towards the back of the building we passed an emergency exit, lit by a red sign. I filed that information away for later. Next to that was another window with a thin ledge. I took the first jump, missed, then jumped again. My feet lined up military style, and I peered in. It was the cat room. Cages stacked four-high lined three of the walls, the entrance door on the fourth. A wooden chair draped with a blanket sat next the door, the "get-to-know-you-station." The cement block walls were painted blue, a stencil of dancing kittens drawn by the ceiling. The false bravado was not lost on me. While most of the cats were asleep in pairs or singly, a few sat at attention, tense and jaded.

"Pssst. This is the cat room. Everyone take a turn, take a look," I ordered as I jumped down.

Sloan went first then landed next to me in a graceful, swift movement. "Do you think this will work?" he
hissed to me under his breath.

"It has to," I said quietly. Then louder, "Minx, did
you spot Rogue?"

"No. His cage is against this wall with the other
cats set to be snuffed," he said, tapping his pointy claws on
the side of the clapboard-sided building. "I've already tried
busting into this window."

"It didn't work?" I asked, knowing full well the
answer.

"No."

"Right answer. Because you had the wrong plan.
That is not my plan."

Minx glowered but kept moving. We only had one
window left to check before we rounded to the front door
to set off our entire plan of action. This window looked
in on an office of sorts, dark and empty. Short of a hidden
employee in the hallways or restroom, that meant we had
gotten lucky; there was only one staffer on deck tonight.
I slipped around the corner to the front of the building to
get a look at him. My initial excitement drained as I saw
the "brute" who must have been the one to grab Rogue.
Wide as a chest freezer and at least 6'11", the man behind
the desk looked like he ate eight pounds of mutton for
lunch. As he scratched at his shaggy black hair, I noticed
his fingers were as think and round as sausages. I retreated
and looked at my band of merry men, and woman.

"Okay. Don't get nervous. This is Step Two," I said
as calm as I could.

I ran through my plan of attack to the rapt audi-
ence.

"Are you high on catnip, Ace?" Minx demanded. "What makes you think that beast of a man won't

grab Sin, Onyx, and Lobo the same way they did Rogue? They'll be tossed in here tonight, we all will, and I'll be skinned!"

"Calm down, Minx. The shelter manager will chase the two cats *outside*, not *inside* with lots of corners and traps," I said. "Onyx, Lobo, you know you need to split up one block down and run up the delegated trees I told you about, right?" They nodded. "Are you confident you can do this? It's especially important."

"We can do this, Ace," meowed Onyx, Lobo swishing her tail in concurrence.

"You can count on us," Onyx agreed. "Cool it, Minx. We got this."

"All right, then. Minx, Sloan, Bob, Kit Kat, and Tiger, you're all with me. Don't forget your roles," I ordered, peering into the window at the thickset shelter keeper one last time before all heck broke loose. The man stretched, flexing a heart-with-an-arrow tattoo on his bicep below his cuffed sleeve. The inscription said, "Yet to be Determined." I took a sharp inhalation. Our jailbreak of an infamous, lawless alley cat was about to begin.

"On the count of three. One, two, three…"

\*\*\*

Onyx and Lobo started scratching and meowing at the door as though they were being chased by a herd of vacuum cleaners. Sin staked out in the shadows, ready for the pursuit to begin. With the others, I laid in wait just on the other side of one of the stone pillars of a friendly-looking lab. The plan seemed to be working; I heard the springs squeak in relief as the burly shelter attendant rose from his chair to attend to the commotion. A giant shadow appeared over Onyx and Lobo, and for a moment I thought they might dart in sheer terror. I can't say I would have blamed them. Like famous detective Sam Spade of the black-and-white era, I don't mind a reasonable amount of trouble but this was ridiculous.

The door swung open and the man stepped out. If you could even call him a man; he was more like a bulldozer. We all slunk a little lower behind the fake canine.

"Hey, kittee, kittees, wanna come inside?" the baritone of false welcoming boomed. "Here kittee, kitteeee."

Just as a massive hand reached out for Onyx, the two cats screeched in his face and bolted like lightning into the frosty, black night. Perfect.

"HEY!" the man bellowed. In hot pursuit, his boots hit the pavement at the speed of a snail traveling uphill. Thankfully his massive, muscular size and bodyweight slowed him down. Behind his slow-moving frame, Sin popped out from the side of the building, hissed loudly, and tore off in another direction, momentarily confusing the already befuddled man.

"Now!" I yelled, slamming myself into the glass door before it could close. Behind me, Sloan and Kit Kat took their brunt of the door's weight while Minx ran inside, shims cradled precariously in his arms.

"Shut the door! Shut the door!" I cried as we all ran inside. We turned and used our might to push the door closed. Relief washed over me as I saw the shelter worker still struggling to catch up to the wily cats that had so rudely upset his evening.

"Minx, shove those shims under the door so he can't open it again. We're going to get Rogue," I said. "Then, weasel up that door and lock it!"

"Who you calling weasel, *cat*?"

"Just do it, *please*!" Sloan shouted as we turned tail and tore down the hallway to the cat room.

Screeching to a halt, we all paused in front of a red door. Hanging on the latch-style doorknob was a kitschy embroidered sign, "Cats for Adoption." I took a giant leap, grasped the latch and pulled down.

"Push on the door!" I said to my crew, dangling. They did an excellent job, and I quickly went swinging into the next room, sliding off and landing in an ungraceful heap on the checked linoleum next to a box of Carl's Cleanest Cat Litter-NOW with less dust! Only a sliver of moonlight shone through the lone window, casting an eerie light on the occupied cages. The room smelled like cleaner and cat dander, dry cat food and loneliness.

"Rogue!" cried Tiger and Kit Kat in unison.

"Is that Rogue?" Sloan asked, looking around. The cages loomed above us, what felt like hundreds of eyes stared at Sloan and I with piqued interest.

"I don't know; does he look like he's about to commit a felony?" I whispered.

Rogue was in a cage on the top row. Death row.

"We've come to get you out!" Minx screamed, tearing around the corner, out of breath.

"Minx! Is the shelter guy back at the door yet?" I shouted.

"No—we've got a little time," he gasped. Quick as a flash, Minx climbed up the cages to Rogue.

"I don't believe this," Rogue, a gigantic black longhair fellow with four white paws, muttered, looking at the ragtag rescue team. Around us, many of the other cats stirred from their slumber and meowed with curiosity. They shoved aside their temporary blankets and institution-provided toys and stuck their paws through the bars. At the realization that this was a break-out, several rattled their latches.

"Me, too, me too, meeeeeeee tooooooo!" some howled. "MEEEWWW!"

I flattened my ears as the piercing cries grew louder.

The distraction was overwhelming, but I brought myself back to the task at hand.

"Sloan, leap up there by Minx, help him loop that string through the pin on Rogue's cage," I directed. Sloan made a giant hurdle and landed on top of the cage, joining Minx in his effort to pull out the pin. Rogue looked at me with interest, then back at the lock. Kit Kat, Bob, and Tiger had begun pawing at several other locks of cats who wanted out. A few, including mothers with kittens or cats with "I'm adopted!" signs told them to lend their devious paws to the others.

"Oh, what the heck," I said, and started helping Tiger and Kit Kat as the lock on Rogue's cage broke free. "Sloan, bring that string over here!" The expired credit card proved useless and laid abandoned on the floor.

"We don't have time for this!" Sloan growled, struggling with his newly-clipped claws on the lock of an orange stripped tabby as he balanced on a second-story cage.

"Quickly! There's just a few left!" Rogue exclaimed, suddenly looming beside me. His enormous size was an ominous presence, and his strength was unrivaled. From the outside, those locks provided no challenge to him what-so-ever. He finished freeing the cats, then shouted, "That window above my cage will open if you turn the lock. Minx! Have that window wide open, and Bob, get these cats *outta here*! I'm goin' to get Frisky."

Frisky? Who was Frisky? Frisky was not part of the plan.

"Who are you talking about?" I asked.

"A dog. I was tryin' to save him in the first place, and I can't leave without him! You with me?" Rouge asked.

"I'm in!" shouted Minx, making quick work of the

window.

Cats shot through the gaping window and into the autumn night.

I jumped like I'd just touched my nose to a light bulb when, from the front, I heard loud pounding and shouting of intense anger.

"HEY!" The shelter worker was back. "HEEEYYY!"

We were out of time.

"Rogue, I hate to tell you, but we have to leave. *Now!*" I exclaimed. More furious pounding boomed from out front.

"No! I won't leave without him," Rogue shouted as he ran out of the door, Minx hot on his tail. I looked at Sloan and sighed. This was bad news for this reporter. I took off after the pair, knowing the angry shelter worker would see us all streaking to the dog ward as he stood assaulting the clear glass door. We might as well confess and hand over our freedom right now. Perhaps we could save him some work and crawl into the cages ourselves.

Rogue and Minx opened the dog door, and the canines woke up with a healthy round of barking, yapping, yipping, and woofing. It was deafening. Beside me, Sloan appeared. I was impressed by his bravery. Behind him came Kit Kat, paper clip still in his teeth.

"What can we do?" he hollered, spitting out the paperclip and surveying the scene as dogs jumped up and down, barking at the top of their lungs. Minx and Rogue worked the lock of the cage holding a small, red terrier mix, presumably Frisky. His pointy ears were alert.

"You guys can't do this, you're gonna get caught. AGAIN!" Frisky scolded in a screechy voice.

"LEMME IN," bellowed the man out front, shaking the door against its hinges. His voice had all the kindness of vaccinations and flea baths.

"We'll never be able to get that dog on top of the cat cages, and out the window," I yelled. "And the front door is barred by a slightly put-out employee!"

"The emergency exit!" Sloan yelled.

"It's too obvious," I said, shaking my head. "We need another distraction."

"Think fast, Ace. What now?" Sloan urged.

I took a second to form a new strategy. I took half a second to tell myself I was certifiably bonkers. I took a split second to put it into action.

"Let these other dogs out. All of them—the big ones first," I ordered, running up to the first cage holding a slim, white German Shepherd-mix pounding to get out.

"If I get you out, you have to help me!" I told the dog. The dog nodded and yapped, his brown eyes pleading for release. His nametag said "Bolt." That should have discouraged me, but it didn't.

Sloan and Kit Kat worked to let more dogs out, but some were happy to stay.

"All right, Bolt. My name's Ace, and I will ride you tonight," I informed him. I once rode on the back of a docile llama. I was hoping this German Shepherd mix would prove similar.

"I'M GONNA GET ALL OF YOU!" the shelter staff man shouted acidly, kicking the outside door with his steel-toe boots.

A number of other odd-sized dogs exited their cages and ran around aimlessly, adding to the chaos. Sloan and the others worked to free the locks of the final few cages. As I wrestled with Bolt's cage, I saw Rogue was successful in freeing his red friend. He climbed onto Frisky's back. As the lock to Bolt's cage burst open, the giant white dog shoved his way out. Grasping with all four paws, I held on as the door swung out and back again.

"Come over here!" I called. Bolt responded well to commands and lined up for me to drop onto his back. "Sorry about the claws," I added as I took hold of his collar. He panted heavily, wound-up and full of energy.

Bark, ruff, bark, ruff.

"SHUT UP!" I hollered. "BE QUIET!"

Ruff, ruff, bark, bark!

Now, historically I get along with dogs, despite their rank odor and lack of behavioral manners. Right now, however, I was ready to send the whole bunch to obedience school.

"SHUT UP Y'ALL!" bellowed Rogue.

Silence.

"You're on, Ace," Rogue said with a smile. I grinned my appreciation.

"Sloan, climb onto the larger dog. That means you, Labrador Sally. Kit Kat, I need you to run out the emergency exit door. The alarm will sound and it will distract the shelter employee away from the front door. As soon as he is gone, I need Minx to unlock the front door. We'll all line up at the door. Then, Minx, I need you to remove the shims. Dogs, pull the door open, and we'll all hustle through quickly but *orderly*. That means Minx will have to get on a dog last."

"And then?" asked Rogue.

"We all run like mad. Meet back at the alley."

Rogue nodded his approval, his paws hugging the scrappy terrier. The two were nearly the same size. The front door continued to rattle and shake. I wondered vaguely if he had his work keys—was the door unlocked already? Was the only barricade standing between our break to freedom those flimsy shims? Would neighbors hear the commotion and call authorities?

"Kit Kat, are you okay with this?" I questioned.

"I can do it," he replied, but I could see the fear in his eyes. With a look of sheer determination, and perhaps before he could change his mind, Kit Kat became a black streak as he ran out of the dog room towards the emergency exit.

Phase Three of our plan was underway.

*** 

"Let's go," I said.

Momentarily, the canines fell silent as our plan went into action. I caught Sloan's eye, his paws clumsily gripping the collar of the black lab. He shook his head in exasperation, but I could see he was amused. Suddenly the alarm sounded; Kit Kat was out the emergency door. The pounding out front stopped. We approached the glass door in an ungraceful dog-cat mix, Minx already unlocking the door. The beefy shelter worker was nowhere in sight. Kit Kat had managed to successfully divert him away.

"This is it! Hurry!" Rogue cried.

"Let's beat it outta here!" Lobo yelled.

"Are we all here?" I shouted as the commotion was steadily building out of my control, looking around at the dogs and cats while tallying up names of our offbeat roster of animals.

"Let's ride!" screamed Rogue as Minx finished with the shims and Frisky pulled at a rope around the door handle. Bolt suddenly took off in a frantic leap to exit the building.

"Steady boy, I'll tell you where to go," I said into his gigantic ear. He didn't seem to hear me as all the bodies of the dogs mashed together, struggling to get out the door all at once. Barking, whining, and yipping erupted at an ear-splitting level. These dogs made Fifi and Fluffi sound like opera singers.

"Ease up, ease up!" I could hear Rogue shouting as fur and ears and tails smashed together. I caught a glimpse of Minx as he held onto a mixed terrier, and even *he* looked a bit concerned.

The cold air hit us all hard as dogs tore off in every direction. I felt the events careening out of my control, but I was powerless to stop them.

"Meet at the alley!" I heard Rogue cry.

"Sloan! Sloan!" I yelled, piercing my claws into the white shepherd in a miserable attempt to get him to slow down. "Bolt! You're going in the wrong direction!"

"I'm not going near THAT!" Bolt hollered. I turned my head and saw the black-haired, husky, angry shelter worker shaking his fist at the animal chaos around him. I wondered if he'd have a job in the morning.

"GET BACK HERE YOU NO GOOD VAR-MITS!" he shouted, his face scrunched into the expression of a man who just had a brick dropped on his toe. "Going back there" did not seem like a sensible option for any of us.

"Kit Kat!" I yelled, frantically searching for his shaggy black coat as my dog bounced along. I hoped that since I hadn't seen him clenched in the staffer's arms, he'd gotten away safely. Faster and faster, Bolt took me away from the shelter, away from Sloan and away from Rogue. It was official, this entire night had gone completely awry.

Bolt pounded pavement and continued to ignore my pleas to slow down. His body heaved with the deep pants of air he took in and out. Finally realizing he had a passenger, Bolt came to a stop a few blocks north of Penny Street. He knelt down, and I jumped off. My body was stiff from panic, and my legs were shaking.

"Thanks, pal," I said genuinely, shaking feeling back into my limbs. He may have led me way off course, but anything south of Canada was better than the enraged fists of the robust shelter guy.

"No problem," Bolt panted, taking in his surroundings.

"You got a place to go?" I asked.

He cocked his head. "I ran away from home a couple days ago. It's time to head back. I knew I shouldn't have left but this rabbit, he kept taunting me. I got lost on his trail," he told me.

"Why didn't your companion come looking for you?"

"I run off a lot, but I've never been caught like this. I always go home," he said. "I'm sure they're waiting for me."

"You should stop that. You're fortunate to have a home to go to," I noted, feeling responsible for his safety. "Are you sure you can get back all right? You have to watch for cars. Don't chase them, either."

"I know. I caught a scent here; I'll be home soon. Thanks, cat," he said, starting to take off. He stopped and turned, looking at me. "Your name is Ace?"

"Yeah."

"What are you, anyway? Some kind of caped crusader without a cape?"

"No. I'm just a reporter."

# 😺 CHAPTER FOURTEEN 😺

After Bolt lollopped into the night, I walked in the direction of Penny Street. My mind was racing and I hoped all of the cats had gotten back safely. I also worried about the well-being of all those cats and dogs we'd freed. For those who were truly homeless—would they know where to go? What would they do?

Rounding the corner of Penny Street, I took a moment to take in my surroundings and made sure I wasn't being tailed by any unsavory characters with heart-and-arrow tattoos peeping out from under their sleeves. It was mid-evening now, the street was quiet. Only the sound of a loud television set blaring through the paper-thin walls of a nearby house could be heard. Richard Simmons was encouraging a spandex-clad crowd to sweat to the seventies.

Entering the secret alley of Rogue, I heard a cacophony of voices. Following them, I found an array of cats surrounding an old milk crate where the manatee-sized Rogue stood, his arm draped casually around a cream-colored long hair with a faux-gem collar. Lady

Diamond. Everyone was celebrating; the big bad wolf was back in town. Minx danced around, handing out bits of jelly donut to hungry felines. Frisky panted with a large grin on his face. I carefully approached, listening to their excited chatter. I was grateful to spot Kit Kat and the others. We were all here. It was a jailbreak miracle. On the outskirts of the group, Sloan spotted me and ran to my side.

"Sloan! Do you know what this is?" I asked.

"Yes, Ace. I believe this is what's called breaking and entering, vandalism, and felony escape," he tallied up on each toe.

"Right, buddy," I said, patting his shoulder. "But we did it. This is a plan that *actually* worked. We freed a cat marked for death."

"You're right," Sloan agreed, smoothing his ears. "Hey, did you get back okay? I thought that lab I was riding was going to career straight into a minivan. With my clipped claws, I could barely hold on."

"The shepherd took me out of the way, but that's all right," I answered, quieting as Rogue called for silence.

"Make way, cats," Rogue ordered. They all parted, became silent, and looked at me.

"Well, look what the cat dragged in," he announced. I stared at him.

Rogue motioned for me to come forward.

I wasn't a dog that would sit up on my haunches, though. I remained seated next to Sloan. Lady Diamond's green eyes sparkled as she examined me, but didn't smile. Sensing my hesitation, Rogue leapt to the ground and walked to me, his gigantic head towering well over mine. He must have Maine Coon mixed in his bloodline.

"Are you Ace?"

"I am Ace."

Offering an outstretched paw that resembled a furry baseball glove, Rogue declared, "I owe you one. Much obliged."

I took his paw and nodded. He watched me, waiting. Sometimes a long pause can be a reporter's best friend.

"You must have good sources to have found me," he finally said.

"I do," I answered, thinking smugly of Ally. "Your reputation precedes you."

"That it does," Rogue asserted, pleased. "But, hey. Don't believe everything you hear. I'm much worse than all that." His cronies laughed, but I didn't. Rouge added, "You look like you mean business."

"I do mean business," I answered. "But first, those cats we freed-where will they go?"

Rogue waved a paw. "No worries. Bob is our homeless coordinator. He'll help find shelter and food, and eventually permanent homes."

I nodded, relieved. "Might I have a word alone?" I asked.

"Certainly, certainly. Walk with me."

Rogue walked in the direction of the entrance to the lair, the same area where Minx had first asked for my help in busting his hero from the pen. That was yesterday; it felt like a lifetime ago. I motioned for Sloan to accompany us, but Minx exploded.

"If he's coming, *I'm* coming!" he demanded insolently.

"Enough, Minx," snapped Rogue.

The weasel cowered at his words and sat down at the entrance in a sulky huff. As I walked by him, his odor reminded me of yesterday's litter box. Lady Diamond sauntered over to join him. I had to question her sense of smell.

"Alright, Rogue. But I'll be right here if you need me," Minx said, glaring at me. It didn't hurt my feelings. "We can go back to not liking each other now," he whispered to me as I passed. I paused.

"Now, Minx. Don't overestimate the situation. We never liked each other."

Minx chewed on that, then shrugged.

Rogue led Sloan and I into the familiar kennel. "This way," he stated as he walked inside, the burlap door covering closing behind us. He paused to scratch just inside the door, his razor-sharp claws glistening in the moonlight.

"That feels good, I haven't had a good scratch in weeks," Rogue groaned. "Whew. That mink is like Velcro to my leg. Don't get me wrong, he's useful and a nice guy and all that, but a cat could use some room to breathe, you know?"

I nodded. He must have meant "room to breathe" literally.

"Can I offer you some catnip? It's pure, uncut," Rogue offered.

"No, thanks, I'm working," I said, omitting the fact that I avoid the stuff all together. Sloan also shook his head.

"Man, does it smell a little fruity in here?" Rogue observed, sniffing the air as he spread out a hit of aromatic catnip.

"I don't know what you're talking about," Sloan said quickly.

"What can I do for you, Ace? Or maybe I should begin by asking what brought you to the wrong side of the tracks, slummin' it in my alley? Ain't you a housecat?"

"Journalist. I live at *The Daily Reporter*."

Rogue eyed me. His pupils dilated as he took in the pile of herb. He flopped inelegantly onto a pillow and peered up at me, motes of dust rising around him like an un-angelic halo.

"You're writing an article, then?" he asked.

"You could say that; but I'm also solving a crime."

Rogue sniffed, then replied, "Heroic. Maybe I should have that sentiment crotched onto a pillow for you."

Uh-oh. Was he mean while under the influence?

"Hardly," I retorted, skipping the chatter and getting straight to the point. "I'm looking for Ruby the Russian. Famous show cat gone missing. I believe she's been cat-napped. I know you know the underground system, Rogue. I helped you. Now I need your help. Tell me who you think might have taken her, pawned her, or sold her."

"Your sources ran dry?" Rogue asked.

"Yes," I admitted. I thought of Ellin and her quilting supplies. "This would be a fairly accessible smuggler. The woman who would have sold her, well, I don't think she's well versed in the world of criminal debauchery."

The cat lolled further back, thinking. "You make a habit of rescuin' animals?" he asked the sky.

"I have a habit of finding the truth. Journalists' creed."

"I don't buy it," he said.

"No problem. It's not for sale."

A tension-filled pause seemed to have us at a draw.

"You're a witty one, huh?" he finally murmured.

"Have I done something to offend you? Like getting your fuzzy tail off death row, maybe?" I quipped.

Rogue's eyes snapped up to my face. "I don't know if you've looked at your paws lately, pal, but you've stepped into quite a mess."

Sloan sat still as a statue. I held my ground. Rogue's dilated eyes met with mine. While I hadn't forgotten Ally's warning about his temper, I grew weary of being treated like a door-to-door encyclopedia salesmen after what I'd just gone through to free the guy. Plus, it was well after my normal bedtime, and no one had saved me any jelly donut. After a pause that lasted approximately two years, Rogue sat up straight and muttered, "Wait a minute. Was it you? You're the reporter who solved the murder this past summer? You involved some cats from The Orange Flamingo."

"Yes. It was me. In the library. With the candlestick," I deadpanned.

"No need for such attitude. I admired that job. Takin' down a full grown man like that? Takes a real set of claws."

"I'm glad you see it that way," I mused.

"I was there," Sloan mentioned. Rogue ignored him.

"Let me tell you something, Ace. Private eye, reporter, 007, whatever you are—you're too witty; that's gonna get you into trouble," Rogue said. He hesitated dramatically. "But I like that."

Rogue stood up, moved over to a ratty, plaid blanket, and flopped down for a change of horizontal position. I adjusted myself to look at him squarely.

He went on, "I don't know your Ruby the Russian. Sure, I've heard of her. Who hasn't? But bein' on the inside, the usual string of gossip has been low. Nonetheless, there's only one guy in Lakeville who would have the skill to steal a high class cat like that, I can tell you that for certain."

My ears pricked up. "Who?"

"Calm down, all in good time, my friend. All in

good time. Let me ask you, does Ruby come from a fancy home with tight security?"

"Yes. Including a vicious guard dog," I confirmed.

"I figured, I figured," Rogue, said nodding. "You've got no real concrete suspects, correct?"

Sloan and I looked at each other.

"One. Maybe," I said. Not to mention Mr. X, the unknown I haven't forgotten. "We think it was an inside job on some level or another."

"Well, cross that person off your list. 'Cause I firmly believe that The Moustache is your guy," Rogue declared.

"The Moustache?" Sloan echoed.

"Yeah, Kramer 'The Moustache' Carter," Rogue nodded.

"I take it this Carter fellow has an admirable collection of facial hair, or perhaps an aversion to razors?" I asked.

"Yeah. Something like that. It's his M.O.," Rogue confided. "He makes Tom Selleck look like an amateur."

Great, something to look forward to.

Rogue continued, "Regardless, Ace, The Moustache illegally runs all the animals. Show cats, minks, ermines, angoras, even some exotics. He once stole some alpacas. Expensive fur and breedin' stock, you know."

"How the heck do you smuggle an alpaca?" I asked, appalled.

"He's just that good."

"All right. What does he do with the animals?" I asked.

"Sells 'em. To the highest bidder."

"How long does that take?"

Rogue mused, "Depends."

"On?"

"How long it takes to find a bidder. Keep in mind these animals are hot. You don't want to hold on too long to somethin' that's hot, do you? You get burned," Rogue explained.

I thought for a moment.

"You think your gem Ruby was already pawned?" Rogue inquired.

"What's your opinion?"

"I'd say no. He's not sellin' her for her fur. He's sellin' her for her show quality. He would need an out-of-state buyer, I'd say. That would take a border run. He only goes on those once a month—the last of the month."

Mentally, I counted down the days to the end of the month; plenty of time.

"Where can I find this 'Moustache' character, Rogue?" I implored.

"Ace, you sure you wanna get your paws in this deep?"

"I'm already up to my ears. I'll keep going."

He gave me a lopsided grin. "Nice, nice." Why did this cat always repeat himself? "I'll tell you this, Ace. You can't just walk up to his door with a basket of cookies and expect he'll turn over the damsel in distress."

"What do I look like, a golden retriever? I figured that."

"Good, good," he answered, unoffended. "The Moustache lives a block past The Orange Flamingo."

Sloan audibly groaned. We were all too familiar with The Orange Flamingo and its less-than-savory crowd.

"He keeps the animals in cages in the basement. The house otherwise looks ordinary. Gray. One story. White trim. Red door. 155 Oregon Street. Enjoy your trip."

Rogue draped a paw over his eyes for a nap. If he

thought this meant our conversation was over, he was wrong.

"Rogue, have you busted animals out of here before?" I pressed.

"Where do you suppose Minx the mink came from?" he murmured over his furry arm.

"Then there's more you can tell me," I said.

"I feel I've told you enough," he said, yawning and getting up to stretch. "I've had a long day. I'm ready for a nap with Lady Diamond. I couldn't sleep worth a darn in the joint."

I shook my head adamantly. "You would be taking a permanent dirt nap if it wasn't for me."

Rogue stopped.

"*What* do you want now?" he mewled tiredly.

"How did you break Minx out of The Moustache's basement?"

He sat down. "Okay, okay. There's a brick. A concrete brick in the basement that's loose. If you're strong enough to muscle it out of the way, you can crawl into the basement. Once you're in, you're on your own. He locks up different animals in different ways. Cages, some with locks, some without. Some animals just run free. It's a riot down there. A real racket."

"How many times have you freed these animals? How can you keep doing this and not get caught?" I marveled.

"You want me to tell you *all* my secrets?"

I gave him a stare that told him I did. He sighed in mock defeat.

"I haven't been successful for that long, my newspaper friend. When I first discovered the place, it was because of a runaway. Kit Kat, the big black fellow out there who you met. He discovered the brick. He was a kitten bein' primed for show, but he was never missed. He led me back, and whenever we could, we let loose anyone we could. The Moustache doesn't have animals all the time; that would be highly suspicious, wouldn't it?"

"Thank you, Rogue. You've been immensely help-ful."

"That finally it? Good, good. Then thank *you*, Ace. Sloan."

Rogue shook both of our paws. Sloan exited the kennel, anxious for some fresh air, I think. The stench of catnip was overwhelming. I turned to Rogue. I still had one last burning question.

"Is your name really Rogue?" I asked quietly.

Rogue looked around for prying ears and whis-pered back, "How did you know?"

"Reporter's hunch,"

"Promise you won't tell?"

"You have my word."

Maybe it was the fact that I'd just rescued this oner-ous alley cat from a death sentence that persuaded him to open up to me. Perhaps I'd gained his trust in sharing my noble mission. Or maybe it was the catnip.

"It's Mr. Mittens," he said. Then he pointed an accusing toe, "Don't judge.

# ❧ CHAPTER FIFTEEN ❧

I considered going to 155 Oregon Street that very night. If not for Sloan's convincing argument that planning over a can of tuna at the office was the best way to go, I would have left on my own.

"What makes you think we'll be successful twice in one night, Ace? Let's go home and draw this out," Sloan proposed.

"Fine, fine," I sighed, shaking my head as I scolded myself for repeating words like our new pal, Rogue. My excursion with the alley cats had gone better than expected, however there was no mistaking the fact that Minx would not be initiating an exclusive "Ace the Cat Fan Club" anytime soon. Kit Kat offered his gratitude before we left, a nice gesture on his part. I supposed he could sympathize with our mission, even if he didn't entirely understand what it was.

"Should we tell Aero what we know?" Sloan wondered.

"No," I said as we walked in the shadows toward

home, the cold wind biting at our heels. Winter was issuing a warning; the frigid season was well on its way. "While I'm confident there's a good chance we'll find Ruby, I don't want him angry that I haven't dropped the case."

I also didn't want to get the dog's hopes up.

\*\*\*

"What's new, pussycat?" Max asked the following morning, waking me with a start. My legs felt stiff and tired, my paws tight and achy. What a night. "You've been pulling an awful lot of all-nighters." He snickered at his own joke.

I purred a moody "good morning" and leapt from my bed on top of the filing cabinet to the floor, slowly approaching my water dish. I was parched.

Max snapped on the desk light, his computer groaning as it came to life. It was a few hours to deadline, and the tension in the office was palpable. One of the sales representatives seemed to have lost some ad copy and was frantically harassing every employee hoping they had seen it. A graphic artist was up in arms because her computer kept crashing whenever she tried to print a sample newspaper page. She looked ready to cry or throw something.

Max, in stark contrast, yawned and began sorting through his email. He must already have his stories in for the morning, I thought groggily, wondering if he'd seek out a cup of coffee and share the cream.

"Here's the morning mail, Max," the secretary said, dropping a small pile onto the overflowing in-tray on Max's desk.

"Thanks, Linda," Max said, picking up the stack without enthusiasm. Jumping to his desk, I peered over his shoulder. Maybe a ransom note? There was the unmistakable appearance of *The Branford Examiner*—the local competition and a shady newspaper to boot—plus a few offers for Max to subscribe to writing workshops, an agenda from an email-frightened city clerk in the next city over, and a small envelope with shaky, scrawled handwriting that no doubt screamed Elderly-Person-Very-Unhappy-with-Newspaper.

"Uh-oh," muttered Max, rolling his eyes and slicing the envelope open with his index finger. "This must be Mr. Mason again."

Mr. Mason was a thick-glasses-wearing gentleman who lived just down the street. He was adamant about weighing in every other day or so on the news, unsteadily writing letters to the editor or just plain demands for the editor to crack on our reporting. While we were all nice to him and tried to respect his freedom of opinion, we also had to tread lightly. If we gave the guy everything he wanted, there wouldn't be any room left for actual news; but it wasn't Mr. Mason scolding *The Daily Reporter* today.

"Huh," Max said, reading the short letter. I followed along over his shoulder as Max read aloud. "Dear Big Shot Reporter, please be advised that missing cats are not news. If you would be so kind, please refocus on larger news items of the day, such as garbage disposal, foot care clinics, and discount sales at the market. Sincerely, Mrs. Louise Bigg."

Mrs. Bigg was clearly a dog person.

Max absent-mindedly pet my head and threw the letter in the direction of the recycling bin near his desk. It hit the brimming stack and slipped under the desk. Max, going back to his email, paid it no heed.

"This is odd…sounds like several animals escaped from the shelter last night. That employee will have some answering to do to the city council next week," Max observed from an email, laughing quietly.

I disguised my surprised gag as an aggressive sneeze and left the office. My paw prints were all over that mess. Venturing into the break room, wanting to put as much space between myself and the accusing email as possible, I investigated the food spread. Finding a slice of day-old bread, I tore it apart while mentally going through the plan Sloan and I had arrived at late last night over canned tuna. Truth be told, it was a sad excuse for a plan. I suspect Phillip Marlowe would be positively ashamed of us if he was around to supervise my lowly, misguided detective skills.

Nonetheless, tonight we would descend upon Kramer "The Moustache" Carter's house, find the movable brick, and—with any ounce of luck—find Ruby there, ready for rescue. Our preparations were hardly complicated; after examining the matter at hand, we found there was truly no way to prepare. Furthermore, we didn't want to involve any other cats. Munching away at the increasingly stale bread, I wondered about everything from Ruby's captivity to the angry letter regarding the reporting on missing show cats. A tap at the window broke my thoughts. Glancing up I saw Ally, precariously perched on the windowsill.

Mouth full and eyes wide, I motioned to the back of the building. Ally quickly nodded and disappeared from sight. Taking a hearty swallow, I quickly licked my forearms and paws, hastily sliding them along my ears and head, trying to tame the flyaway tufts of fur. I darted to the back of the building, expertly avoiding the bustle of feet scrambling to meet deadlines. Bursting through the mail slot, I looked around for the blonde feline.

"Ally?" I whispered.

"I'm here," she called, appearing lovely as ever from behind a dumpster.

"What are you doing here?" I asked.

I led Ally to the gas station and convenience store next door where a rickety picnic table sat under the changing leaves of a gigantic oak and towering maple, nearly devoid of all the colors of fall. A blue-black starling tugged at a reluctant worm in the hardening ground.

"You can't go off to see a guy like Rogue and leave me hanging, Ace," Ally reprimanded lightly.

"Right. I'm sorry," I apologized, dipping my head with shame. "I've been wrapped up in the story and didn't even think to follow up with you."

"Well? What happened?"

I didn't want to confess to her that Sloan and I had foolishly dove headlong into a late night cell-busting rendezvous, so I hesitated.

Ally knew me too well. "Oh, no, Ace. What did you do?"

"Am I that obvious?"

"More than you know."

I filled her in on the details, including my initial meeting with Minx and the alley cats, the subsequent shelter break with a less-than-friendly manager and finally our one-on-one conversation with Rogue himself. Ally slowly shook her head.

"Do you want to be in Rogue's debt, Ace?" Ally asked.

"Rather, I believe he is still in my debt. I saved him from a grave future," I reminded her.

"I know, but Rogue doesn't exactly play fair," Ally said. "What are your next plans?"

Again, I hesitated.

"Tell me."

"Sloan and I are going to The Moustache's place tonight. I think Ruby is there. She has to be. It's been days, and no ransom note. The Moustache doesn't do ransoms. All the pieces fit! He sounds like the culprit. Maybe I can get to Ruby before he sells her off out of state."

Ally appeared unconvinced.

"How many times have you leapt into something like this without knowing the consequences?" she asked.

"Well, once. Twice. Okay, three times. Four, if you count the fourth," I muttered. I could have kept going, but the look on Ally's face told me I didn't need to. I felt as guilty as the cat that swallowed the canary.

"Rogue is bad news. The Moustache is worse, and Ace, you know all about bad news," Ally pleaded with me. "Do you think that The Moustache isn't onto Rogue? Who is to say there won't be a trap there waiting for you? Something set for Rogue but that snaps on you instead? Do you suppose that The Moustache would let you go? Or that Rogue would come to save one of your nine lives?"

"I'll be careful with The Moustache. Never trust a man who over-grooms," I mentioned, "besides, I'll have Sloan with me."

Ally frowned at my sarcasm., my usual defense mechanism. "All the more reason to avoid this all together. Don't put him in harm's way. I know you don't mean to, Ace, but accidents happen."

Ally's reasoning struck a chord deep inside of me. That *was* the reason I hadn't wanted to go behind the headlines into direct, detective crime-solving again; I didn't want anyone to get hurt. Ally knew that better than anyone. It was her little brother who suffered this summer, after all. Was I acting reckless to get to the bottom of this story? I cleared my throat.

"I'll leave Sloan home. But me, I've done this be-fore, Ally; I can do it again. It's a reporter's job to—"

Ally cut me off.

"You're a black cat. You can't keep getting this lucky. I'm not here to stop you, Ace. I'm here to warn you. The other side of the tracks is the other side for a reason. I can hardly complain about your actions this summer. Solving the mystery not only set an innocent woman free, but you also found the real killer and somehow managed to bring Peter and I into a loving home in the process," Ally rushed her words, "but now it's time to take care of you. Be yourself."

"That hasn't worked out so great for me."

Ally sighed.

"What about Ruby?" I urged.

"It think it's safer for everyone if you don't get involved in solving this mystery. Let the humans handle this."

I answered her with conviction, "I can't do that."

Ally nodded her consent, "I'm just concerned."

"I appreciate that, Ally, I truly do. You've been a great friend. I'm sure you'll understand that I have to do this tonight, even if that means coming face to face with The Moustache."

"There's nothing I can say to change your mind?" she asked.

"I sincerely doubt that. Go home to Peter," I said as I gently placed a reassuring paw on her shoulder. Ally looked ready to cry, but she bit her lip and agreed.

"Don't let me down, Ace," she said as she walked away, her blonde tail swishing behind her.

***

Ally's words hung over me throughout the day like a rain cloud. Was it indeed time for me to stop playing detective and crawl back behind my byline? Trouble was, I've been a lot in my lifetime, but I've never been a quitter. Whether or not I ever ventured back into the realm of detective work was a figment of speculation, but I had to finish what I'd started. This story needed an ending.

Determined, to keep this as clean as possible, I visited Sloan's apartment across the way. True to my word to Ally, I'd leave him home. I found him out back, sprawled on the hot sidewalk with his limbs out like he'd been dropped from an airplane.

"Still trying to shake the smell, buddy?" I asked.

"Ace! I didn't hear you walk up. I thought we weren't meeting until later?"

"Yeah. About that," I began.

"What?"

"I need to go alone," I sighed.

"Okay."

"I have to do this, don't try to stop me."

"I wasn't going to."

"This is something I've started, and I have to finish it, no matter what you say."

"Sure."

I paused, "Wait. Aren't you going to try and stop me?"

"No. I figured you were ready to go on this alone. You tend to do that, you know? Go all solitude and attitude toward the end of your journeys."

"I do?"

"Well, yeah. Plus, I have a date tonight. It turns out Peaches doesn't mind dirt mingled with fruity essence," Sloan said.

I sensed he was lying.

"Great, then," I said anyway, "I'll let you know how it goes. With any luck, I'll be writing about Ruby's happy reunion with her family tomorrow morning."

Sloan smiled, looking apprehensive despite his assurance that I should go it alone.

"Be careful, Ace. The Moustache sounds like he could be a bit hairy."

# CHAPTER SIXTEEN

The Moustache.

The disturbing name alone conjured all sorts of images as I prepared for my evening by my lonesome. A man nicknamed for his epic proportion of facial hair could not equate to a friendly neighborhood Nobel Peace Prize winner.

*The Daily Reporter* dwindled down to just an employee or two, finishing up some work before leaving for the day. Despite the morning drama, the paper successfully made it out the door yet again. While the quiet usually lulled me into a sense of relaxation, it grated on my nerves today. Part of me half-heartedly hoped the fax machine would groan to life and spit out a fax, announcing Ruby's safe return home, no thanks to me, but eliminating the need to show at The Moustache's lair. However, it remained resolutely silent.

Too wired to sleep and not ambitious enough to start any other projects, I left the newspaper, absent-mindedly heading for downtown. I couldn't stand the fax machine looking at me like that anymore.

It was absolutely dark outside, the stars smattered and glittered across the ink black sky. As I walked I thought of Aero, of Madeline and Ellin, and of course, of Ruby. Had Aero truly given up hope? Was Madeline also on the verge? Was Ellin actually hiding something, her motives dark and sinister? What if Ruby *had* left of her own accord? Was my nosing around going to answer all these questions? Reporting never failed to solve my most common mysteries before, but rarely had so much been at stake.

Stopping on the sidewalk, I eyed the quilt shop. Yellow lights burned warmly inside. I could see a few women picking through yards of fabric while Ellin stood stoically behind the counter, looking drained and agitated, not unlike yours truly. I watched as she removed a pill from a bottle alongside her purse and swallowed it, cringing slightly. She probably had a killer headache, another late night for the small business owner. She didn't look guilty, she just looked tired.

Three stores down, I sighed as my eyes caught a poster curling at the edges, pleading for information on Ruby the Russian, still gone without a trace. I kept moving.

Anne's Coffee Cup was closed for the day, but I wondered if Lily was about. There was nothing wrong with my life at the moment that a jelly donut and a cup of cream couldn't fix. As I sauntered alongside the brick building, I heard several voices coming from the back. Did Lily have friends over? Curious, I decided to quickly investigate. My surprise intensified when I rounded the corner and found Lily in the company of none other than Sloan, Ally, and Peter. Peter barreled into me, causing me to stagger back a couple of feet.

"Ace! Ace! Hiya! How are you? Are you well? Are you on another case? How do you do it all? Have you heard about Snow White's seven dwarves joining Broadway? Could be a story idea…"

I took a beat to think.

"Okay, who gave the kid sugar?" I asked as Peter rambled at an alarming speed.

My confusion at their gathering was transparent. Lily looked sheepish.

"Ace, darling. I pulled it out of Sloan this morning. And then Ally stopped by, they told me what you were up to tonight, and, well, you can't do this alone," she explained, coming over to put her paw on my shoulder. "We were about to come down to the newspaper and tell you that we're coming with. No matter what you say."

"I thought you were okay with this," I said in Sloan's direction, "I thought you had a date with Peaches."

Sloan shrugged his shiny gray shoulders and gave me a sly grin. "It's nothing that can't wait. I couldn't let you go by yourself to face The Moustache, not really," he said.

"We're all coming," Lily quipped. Just as I began to open my mouth to put my foot down on their intention of going with, she interrupted, "I know how you feel about this, Ace, but we are your friends, and no one knows that neighborhood better than these two."

Ally smiled kindly and nodded. Peter paced between all of us, buzzing conspiracies just below his breath at the approximate rate of a mouse hopped up on Pixie Sticks. I noticed a jelly donut in front of him, all the sugary icing licked clean.

"I don't know what to say," I muttered.

Sloan looked at me at over his cup of warm milk as

Lily topped it off with cream. Steam slowly rose in front of his face. "We can pull this off quickly and cleanly. You know, like how I ruined the new pantyhose that Mary just put on when she was running late for work this morning," Sloan mused, lapping. "It took like, one hole and they just completely unraveled. Quick and clean! ZIP! "

Max didn't wear pantyhose, so I didn't know how to respond to that.

Lily topped off Ally's cup of milk and turned to me, "Would you like a cup of warm cream?"

"Make it a double, Lily. Neat."

She raised her eyebrows but obliged. I wrapped my tail around the warm cup. Lily pushed a jelly donut towards me, I licked the icing.

The warmth was welcome in the frosty October evening. I agreed with Sloan, my mind still slightly shocked at the turn of events.

"We go right for the windows tonight. Check out the scene, approach the house, leap into a back window and locate The Moustache," I suddenly asserted, feeling the sugar kick in. "Once we pinpoint his location, we locate the brick. Move it. Move in."

"We'll find Ruby and be on our way. Easy cheesy," Lily said while she smiled over her skim milk, her fur glossy even under the dim glow of the back porch light.

"...didn't think Sleepy could sing, I'm sure Doc can't hold a tune, wonder if Rapunzel ever made it into acting? Or is that Hollywood?" Peter continued to rant, his hair sticking out in unkempt tufts in every direction.

I did love these guys.

As Sloan reached for another refill, I scratched my ears and thought hard. Could I still ditch them? While truly touched by their gesture, I couldn't help but hesitate at their instance to tag along. Ally had been right earlier, this was a perilous venture. Now here she was, risking herself and her brother. We knew that the local pound had plenty of vacancy this evening.

"Ace! Are you listening?" Sloan broke into my thoughts, an empty cup before him.

"Huh? What did you say?"

"Ellin is working late. Do you still think she might have something to do with this? Maybe she's The Moustache's girlfriend," he said.

"Oh, well, I'm not sure," I coughed. Ally looked doubtful over her second cup.

"I think he runs solo," she offered as she lapped, "though he does have a sister."

"I suggest we don't cross Ellin off our list, though," Sloan said.

"I suggest we stop drinking milk and cream and get moving," I said abruptly, my mind made up. There was no way I'd get away with this on my own. They knew, after all, exactly where to find me. "We can't accomplish anything if we're in the litter box all night."

"You're right, Ace. Let's get going. Peter? Remember what we talked about?" Ally questioned her little brother.

"Not to approach pumpkins that I believe are weapons of mass destruction?"

"No," Ally said patiently, "about tonight. Staying quiet, out of the way, and safe. You must listen to me at all times."

Peter nodded so fast that the features on his tiny face blurred.

"Okay, gang. Let's *all* stay safe," I said as I lead the way.

It was such a darn shame that I rarely listened to myself.

\*\*\*

We all fell into silence as we stuck to the back alleys and made our way towards the not-so-nice part of Lakeville. Our sugar-fueled bodies spurred us on, countering the nippy autumn air. Tails held high, we careened through the neighborhoods with gardens long sent to bed, surfaces covered with straw and mulch for the long winter ahead. A few cars drove by on the main road, their headlights casting temporary flashes of light over our journey, then drenching us in darkness once again. As neatly trimmed lawns alongside paved sidewalks gave way to crumbling pavement and paint-peeling houses, I reminded myself that we had arrived on the proverbial other side of the tracks. The sidewalk literally ended here; disheveled houses were smaller and duller somehow. There were no sweetly planted flower boxes to tend to, no white picket fence to paint each spring.

It was a good neighborhood for bad manners.

A figure of a giant bird loomed in the darkness ahead: The Orange Flamingo, the trailer park's mascot, a giant, overgrown lawn ornament that flickered and buzzed. I imaged that at one time, in all its original glory, the bird had been pink but years of harsh sunshine and hard living had turned its plastic to a washed-out shade of orange. I let out a visible shudder thinking how Ally and Peter had formerly lived there, just a few short months ago.

Refocusing, I gathered my crowd closer together and asked everyone to read the faded street signs in search for our Oregon Street destination.

"No need, Ace. I know right where to go," Ally said as she took the lead, her blonde face glowing slightly orange as we walked on past The Orange Flamingo's decrepit trailer houses. I fell into step behind her. She picked up the pace, seeming to mimic the agitation that I felt building as the task at hand grew closer. Another two blocks down, Ally turned right and stopped near a bench missing a few slats in a weed-choked lawn.

"There," she said, pointing past a faded pick-up truck. Just as Rogue had described, the ramshackle, gray house had a red door and scuffed white trim. The grass was brown and overgrown, devoid of any sleeping gardens. The house looked dark and dank. Shades were drawn in every visible window. The short rubble driveway, leading to a doorless garage, was vacant.

"Sloan?" I asked softly.

"Yeah?"

"What do you think?"

"Let's circle around back. Look for a light in a window," he said after a moment.

"Sounds good. Okay, Lily? Peter?"

"Right on, Ace," Peter whispered.

"All's good," Lily said.

Slinking into the shadows, the five of us hunched closer to the ground as we came closer to the yard of The Moustache. It was jarringly silent. Working at a newspaper had groomed me to be accustomed to a certain level of noise and the lack thereof put me on edge more so than the sound of an inappropriate polka band. Circling to the back of the house, I was disappointed to find all of the windows had shades or blankets draped over the glass. There was no way to see inside. Great.

"Now what?" hissed Sloan.

"Did anyone see a crack of light? Anything at all?" I asked. I couldn't pick up on any distinct animals smells. It *all* smelled.

"LOOK!" cried Peter, "Another cat!"

We all turned to see.

Peter's hair was on end, his back raised, eyes wild.

I furrowed my brow. Peter had found a shard of broken glass, leaning against the shaky foundation of the house. He was seeing himself.

"Um, Peter?" I ventured.

"Hey, fella!" hissed Peter, prancing back and forth by the mirror. "Stop doing that! You think you're funny, huh?"

"Peter, hon," Ally tried.

"You talkin' to me? I said, are you talkin' to *me*?" Peter taunted himself.

"Omigod. This is going to go on all night, Ace," Sloan groaned. "Give it a rest, Peter, will ya?"

Peter would not. He continued to be dazzled by the mimicry of the identical blonde kitten. He barred his teeth, closed his mouth, barred his teeth, closed his mouth.

I ran up and pushed the mirror over with my paw. Peter snapped out his trance and looked at me. Everyone shook their head. Peter simply shook, his body still vibrating from the sugar jolt and unpleasant mirror interaction.

"Stay here. I have an idea," I said to them all. "I think the front door had a dog flap."

"Pfft! I'm not staying anywhere!" croaked Lily, hot on my tail.

"Fine. Sloan, stay with Ally and Peter, and try to poke around—quietly!—for that loose brick," I urged.

Sloan nodded, and thankfully the brother and sister didn't mind helping.

"And for cripes sake, stay away from any other mirror shards," I mumbled over my shoulder. My best friend gave me a paws up.

Treading silently to the front stoop, I surveyed the crumbling concrete and eyed the front door. Sure enough, a small dog door hung loosely at the bottom, the rubber flap limp. I looked at Lily, pointed to my chest, then to the door. Her green eyes grew wide and she shook her head adamantly. I put up my paw to reassure her, then leapt deftly to the stoop while Lily looked on in dismay. I circled my paw in the air and pointed to my ear. She took the hint and appraised the scene, listening for anything out of the ordinary. She gave me a curt nod, and I put my ear to the flap. It smelled like a dirty, dirty dog. Beyond that, the scents I picked up were masculine and off-putting, like cologne derived from a putrid musk ox. I couldn't hear a single sound. No electronics, no conversation, and no mammals breathing.

Glancing quickly back at Lily, I turned my attention back to the door and put one eye up to a small crack where the door met the frame. Unable to see anything, I hooked the flap with my dew claw and slowly pulled it aside. One-quarter of an inch gave me enough room to dart my superior vision around the room. The Moustache had less discernible decorating taste than a thrift shop; a dirty kitchen appeared just beyond the living room, linoleum patched and peeling. An under-stuffed, brown velvet couch sat squat and sad in the middle of the room directly in front of an ancient television set that could double as a boat anchor. The orange shag carpeting was littered with empty beer cans and overflowing ash trays. Besides a few dog-eared smutty magazines, the room was empty and dark. I let go of the rubber door and backed away.

"I don't think anyone is home," I whispered.

Lily signed in relief, "Let's find the others."

Doubling back to the rear of the residence, we found Ally and Sloan near a covered basement window. Peter was pacing and bickering with himself, which, oddly enough, was perfectly normal.

"This is the brick, Ace," said Ally as she motioned to a cement block roughly twelve inches across and eight inches high. All around it cement crumbled, giving the general appearance of instability.

"Have you tried to wrestle it yet?" I asked Sloan. He shook his head. "Good. Let's you and I try together. I didn't spy anyone inside, it's silent as a tomb. I think we're alone."

Ally looked visibly relieved.

Positioning ourselves on either side of the brick, Sloan and I tried to grasp the corners.

"Curse these shorn claws!" Sloan mewled.

Exerting ourselves as the other cats looked on, Sloan and I worked at the brick, slowly but surely moving it a few millimeters at a time. We grunted and groaned; this was about as fun as hearing about the circulation manager's tonsil removal surgery last week. We pulled and pulled, breathing hard. The sound of brick scraping on brick filled the air and dust rose, making me sneeze. Lily and Ally looked on anxiously.

"Just a few more inches," I breathed. Sloan, his face screwed up in concentration, winked as we kept working at the concrete. The brick suddenly fell forward with a satisfying thud, landing askew on the ground. Sloan and I exchanged wide-eyed looks as we peered beyond the hole, and into the basement.

Empty.

Dark, unbelievably dark, but no doubt empty.

The story had finally run cold.

***

My shoulders slumped forward as I stared unbelievingly into the yawning abyss. A musty smell hovered in the air.

"What is it? What is it?" Lily hissed. Ally appeared anxious. Even Peter had fallen completely quiet.

"Nothing. Absolutely nothing," I said, squaring my

shoulders despite my obvious disappointment.

Lily pushed Sloan aside and peered in.

"It's as though every corner is empty. Do you think he got caught recently? Got scared?" she asked no one in particular.

I shrugged in a noncommittal way.

"This means nothing," Sloan said, seeming to read my thoughts. "Rogue knows The Moustache is an illegal animal runner. We just have to go back and ask him where Ruby would have gone after this, that's all."

I shook my head obstinately. "No, no. This was it. If Ruby isn't here, and Ellin doesn't have her, then Aero must be right. She's gone on her own free will."

"I'm not so sure, Ace," Ally began.

"But earlier today, you said—"

Ally cut me off, "I know what I said Ace, but I was wrong. I was trying to talk you out of coming here. You've been acting reckless, and I wanted to stop you. It appears, though, that The Moustache is long gone. Ruby could still be out there. She could still need your help. What if he took her on an early run? An early sale? What if someone *else* did?"

"Yeah, Ace. What about Mr. X?" Sloan asked.

"Mr. X?" Lily implored, trying with all her body weight to shove the brick back into its rightful place.

"Never mind right now. Let me help you," I said.

The three of us pushed the brick back into its home and looked at each other. Everyone bit their tongues, waiting for me to make a declaration. Their fearless leader, suddenly out of direction.

"Look, I appreciate you all coming with me to-night. It was brave and bold," I said. "I want you all to head back home now. I need some time to clear my head."

As they all began to protest, I dipped my head and

repeated, "I just need a moment alone to think about all this. Okay? I'll see you soon."

With a collective sigh, they each filed past me, giving encouraging pats or smiles. Ally lingered an extra moment.

"You'll solve this, Ace. I believe in you."

Normally, words like that would have warmed my soul. At the moment, however, they just made me feel like a total, dismal failure.

"Thanks, Ally."

\*\*\*

Watching them go, I let my frustration and failure take over. I felt like I was some stupid dog chasing my tail, going nowhere fast.

This was a real fiasco. It wasn't just my time and hide I risked, it was my friends' too. I needed to stop slumming in bad neighborhoods, playing the dashing detective, and leave these matters to the human police. It was that simple.

I meandered to the front of The Moustache's house again, my thoughts overtaking better judgment. Finding myself on the front step, I turned and looked up at the empty house. Where had The Moustache gone? Was he still running animals? Ruby aside, it was a story in and of itself. Perhaps I should try to arouse Max's reporter instinct; he was better equipped to handle situations like this than I was, though surely I'd be by his side. I could still be useful. I could still be good, even if I was a shoddy detective.

Just then, a jolt ran through my body as though I'd walked too close to an electric fence. I crashed back to planet earth. A sense of doom loomed over me as I realized that someone was there. I turned and looked up.

Right into the leering and overgrown face of The

Moustache.

If vehemence had a face, this was surely it.

"Meow?"

"Sorry, I'm all out of sugar," he growled menacingly. His voice was rough, like a dog before he horks up the dinner he ate too fast.

The general appearance of The Moustache made last night's tattooed shelter manager look like a fuzzy teddy bear. The Moustache was aptly titled; his legendary handlebar facial hair deserved its own zip code. Untidy and scrawny, The Moustache had a thatch of brown hair that couldn't rival what consumed his upper lip. His pants were blue plaid, paired with a flamboyant purple shirt. If the situation wasn't so serious, it would have been downright comical.

Making a face like he'd just smelled a big pile of dog doo, The Moustache gripped his grocery bag stacked with Hungry Guy frozen dinners with one hand and reached for me with the other. My back was against the door, his gangly frame attempted to cover any angle of escape. The only way out appeared in, and there was no way I was going *in*. I panicked; as the hairy fingers came closer to my face, I immediately bared my teeth, hissed and struck, claws extended to their full extent. I made full contact, silently thanking Max for not cutting them in recent months. My hairy foe recoiled, his moustache independently climbing upward in an angry grimace. I seized the opportunity to hiss loudly and slash a second time.

"OW! You darn flea bag!" his gravelly voice exclaimed, dropping his sack of frozen goods as he grasped his bleeding hand. His expression conveyed his ability to commit cold-blooded cat murder. It was prime time for me to clear off. For the record I've never had a single flea, much less a bag of them.

With a giant leap, I overtook the toppled brown bag and strewn grocery items, trying to tear off into the night. I couldn't, my claws grabbed nothing but air as I felt myself falter and slam to the ground. Someone had grabbed my tail, preventing my timely get-away.

What *was* this? Kick-the-Cat Tuesday?

Craning my neck, I saw a wiry female with a head of brown hair that could have only been styled by a weed-whacker. She had a single eyebrow that seemed to stretch across the entire expanse of her face like a bushy caterpillar. She tried hard to hold onto my tail with two bony hands. I hissed and growled, panted and spit, finally flipping onto my back to face my unibrow attacker.

"You save me a piece after you're done with him!" The Moustache shouted with more dignity than a man in plaid pants deserved. He fumbled with the door lock with his still-bleeding appendage.

"Hold still!" the nasty woman growled with mutiny in her voice, her hands getting an astonishingly good hold of my throat. "There's more than one way to skin a cat, Mr. Kitty,"

What a fine time to use *that* analogy. It fueled my survival instincts; I curved my spine to one side then the other, ultimately coming up off my back and slashing blindly into the face of the woman towering over me. Her mistake was not restraining my best weapons—my feet. My claws didn't fail me as they pierced her soft cheek, but it wasn't enough. I could feel the breath in my neck quickly depleting. Now, I didn't hold back; I walloped her again, my claws raking across her face. This was no cat scratch, it was a full-on gash. The lady clenched her teeth and howled like a banshee, releasing me to grasp her fresh wound.

I hit the ground running, the air returning in ragged

gasps to my lungs. I ran as though I had stolen something. I ran as though I'd just met the local vet at the mini mart. I ran as though there was no tomorrow. The angry bellows of the woman finally faded as I darted through bushes and trees, across backyards, around swing sets and empty clothing lines. My heart beat faster and faster, the reality of the last few moments catching up to me. Thank goodness the others already left.

Out of breath and shaking like a Chihuahua, I stopped for air alongside a nice yellow house a block away from downtown. The azaleas, crisp and brown, provided nice shelter as I recovered. My breaths came and went in ragged gasps and I kicked myself in the tail for being so stupid. Never, ever, assume the house of a known criminal is vacant and without threat, I scolded myself. The Moustache and his companion were not just from the wrong side of the tracks, oh, no. You had to keep going past the wrong side of the tracks, slightly past crazy and somewhere alongside the haunted graveyard you might be getting close to these villains.

Cripes, that was too close.

Satisfied that I was breathing properly and not being followed, I composed myself and made my way towards Anne's Coffee Cup. I knew there was a chance Sloan and Lily were still hanging around, hopefully having switched to water at this late hour. Sure enough, there they were, talking quietly beneath the back door light. Their chatter halted abruptly when they spotted me. I stood up straight and tried to look indifferent as I approached.

"Oh, my gosh! Ace! What happened to you?" exclaimed Lily, rushing to my side. Sloan's eyes registered shock as they scanned me. I realized my fur was a bit ruffled. I pointlessly tried to smooth it.

"Where are Peter and Ally?" I asked, fear rising in

my belly.

"They're inside, spending the night. Their companion is out of town," Lily replied. "But what *happened?*"

I sighed with relief that everyone was all right and filled in the two felines on my meeting with the smarmy Kramer "The Moustache" Carter and his none-too-lovely sidekick after they left. The words rushed out of me and I was glad to be rid of them. Truthfully, I was ready to forget the entire encounter.

"Oh. My. Goodness," Lily said in staccato-style. She pushed an uneaten cinnamon roll aside, joining a paperback romance where a tanned cowboy was lassoing a muscle-bound stead. A busty milk maid looked on in wonder.

Sloan shook his head in disbelief. "I'm sorry, Ace. I *knew* I should have stayed behind."

"No, Sloan. You did the right move. I wanted everyone to get back safely, and you made sure of that. Besides, I'm fine. Those two are obviously morons. I can't believe they ever managed to smuggle animals illegally," I laughed unconvincingly.

We all chewed on that false statement for a while in silence.

Sloan looked doubtful at my casual dismissal of tonight's fight and flight for my life but didn't say another word, possibly because Lily looked slightly seasick. I hugged and thanked her, asking her to please avoid telling Ally and Peter about my unfortunate meeting with The Moustache clan. With that, Sloan and I headed off in the direction of our respective homes. Tonight, I would go home to Max's warm bed. Out of earshot of the coffee house, I turned to Sloan.

"Making friends with a weasel and orchestrating a jailbreak at the shelter was evidently entirely without benefit," I mused. "Was I ever scratching up the wrong tree."

The city around us appeared dark and vacant. Windows, like eyes without anybody home, sightlessly watched our plight.

"Honestly, Ace. What are we going to do next?" Sloan asked. I could hear the dejection in his voice. It mirrored my own feelings, which I kept closed off inside.

"I don't know, pal. I just don't know."

## 🐾 CHAPTER SEVENTEEN 🐾

After the futile stake out at the alleged hideout of The Moustache, I hung around home like a lazy housecat and still didn't feel any closer to solving my crime as I was to launching a successful detective franchise. I went to work Thursday.

Addled and confused, I laid low in the newspaper office, assisting Max with stories focusing on the recent election. New faces elected onto the Lakeville City Council distracted me only for a moment before my thoughts drifted right back to the stunningly cold eyes of Ruby the Russian's photograph, still staring at me from a "Pending Story" file atop Max's desk.

She was still missing.

I had not been in contact with Aero, Sloan, or anyone. I had not stalked Ellin, and I had not pursued a Mr. X with a motive. It was unlike me, one minute hot on a story, and the next to let go so quick. There was only one explanation, and I had a hard time coming to terms with the reality of it: I was out of clues.

Normally I would revel in a quiet day at the office. I'd lounge on Max's lap with my head in the crook of his arm while he typed, or I'd spread out in my bed atop the filing cabinet for a long nap while the day went on without me.

I felt too useless to enjoy such luxuries today.

There was a gentle knock at the door.

"Sorry to disturb you," Linda apologized as she gave Max an early copy of tomorrow's paper and a stack of letters.

I was already seriously disturbed.

The mail stack contained no indication that a ransom letter for Ruby's return was out there. It wasn't coming.

Max scratched behind my ears and made another keen observation on some of the missing fur from my tail.

"I wish I knew your adventures, Ace," he sighed.

Sometimes, I wish he knew, too.

***

It was late in the night and I was asleep at home. Dreaming. Dreaming wearily of stacks of newspapers falling down all around me. I darted in and out of the newsprint, avoiding the ever-increasing stacks that grew by the minute. The newspapers were angry with me for not doing my job and threw insults at me. Squirming in my slumber, my dream continued, and I ran to the half-full bag of Kuddly Kitty Krunchies to try and escape inside but ended up in the always overflowing recycling box alongside Max's desk instead. Crouching down, I tried to avoid the accusing tone of the newspapers that hollered at me to be a more responsible reporter. Just as I was about to be buried in articles of new building projects and city leaders taking charge, I spotted something.

It was a clue.

My eyes popped open. I may be a good reporter outwardly, but my reporter skills were awful in my own life. I ran all the way to the newspaper office. Through the mail slot, I jetted and skittered into Max's office. Jumping to his desk, I slipped on a few stacks of paper before pawing on the lamp. Squinting against the sudden glow, I leapt down to the recycling box, then moved over to a forgotten and discarded letter.

The letter from Mrs. Bigg.

It took me until this moment, but now I remembered; Mrs. Bigg was *not* a dog person. She was a cat person. So much so that she was often referred to in whispered tones as "The Kooky Cat Lady" during Commission on Aging Committee meetings. It was at these meetings that she would occasionally appear to register an opinion, her flowered housecoat covered in cat hair of every color and texture. It was rumored she took in each and all strays that came her way, that she cared for each feline as though it were her own child. So why would Mrs. Bigg scold us for attempting to reunite Ruby with her own dear family? Why, indeed.

Why? Unless Mrs. Bigg had already fallen in love with her?

***

The next morning dawned cold but bright. I left the office through the backdoor mail slot before Max and the front office staff arrived, anxious to follow my new lead. Before leaving the back parking lot, I noticed that Farfel had been by, the scent of his furry head rubbed on my mail slot as a message. I made a mental note to fill him in at a later date. Hopefully, by then, I'd have solved the crime.

I had Mrs. Louise Bigg's address from her envelope and knew that she lived in a tiny house near the library, just five blocks away from downtown in one of the older housing districts of Lakeville. She often spoke of her abode to the Commission, reminding them that independent seniors living on their own could use some help every fall and spring with yard clean up. I held my tail high and trotted like a detective hot on the trail.

This was it; this *had* to be it.

The usual morning traffic filled the streets as people left their homes for school and work. A Friday, everyone seemed to have an extra burst of energy in their step as they looked forward to the weekend. A renewed feeling of determination filled me as well.

Nearing Mrs. Bigg's neat, mauve-colored home, I rested beside a plastic pinwheel in the neighboring yard. Her house was homey-looking. Flower boxes were filled with decorative fall leaves and gourds. The sidewalk leading to her front porch was neat and trim and the porch itself had cushioned wicker furniture flanking the door. Her mailbox featured a striped tail in back, a painted cat's smiling face in front. Through the living room window I spotted several tabbies on the wide windowsill, languishing in the morning sunshine, their bodies no doubt limp and relaxed in the warmth. Behind lace curtains, I detected movement. Mrs. Bigg was likely awake and busy with the morning feedings of her many cats. I idly wondered if the roles were reversed, would cats with houses take in stray old ladies? Hmm. Probably not.

Approaching Mrs. Bigg's humble home, I was careful not to be seen. I had to decide how to approach the situation at hand. The back porch was uncovered, a trough-sized bowl there overflowing with Kuddly Kitty Krunchies with salmon-flavored x-bites. There must have been a sale on the stuff; Max recently stocked up as well, much to my dismay. On the other side of the porch was a dog-house sized box, lined with straw and flannel. It occurred to me

that this was an outdoor shelter for homeless cats, perhaps
for feral felines that she could not yet coax inside. It was
kind of her, I thought tenderly.

"Okay, babies! Momma has to visit the pharmacy
and market! You behave while I'm gone."

The high-pitched call of Mrs. Bigg's voice alerted me to take immediate cover under the porch, lest I be
taken in and force-fed. I heard her light footsteps above
me, followed by the sharp thump of her cane. I looked up
through the slats and saw her orthopedic shoes shuffling
across, aided by her rubber-tipped walking device. Her
flowered purse, clashing wildly with her cat-pattern housecoat, swung from her other arm. Her blue hair was teased
into a rounded poof on her head, and fuzzy earmuffs
protected her ears from the cold. Entering the carport, I
heard her boat-sized sedan roar to life. This was no hapless
old lady. I admired her for her strength, stamina, and inde-
pendence at such an old age. Watching her carefully back
out of the short driveway, she took off down the street at a
speed exceeded only by passing butterflies.

With Mrs. Bigg safely out of sight, I ventured onto
the porch landing. The door did not have a dog or cat flap.
Looking from side to side, I observed two windows low to
the ground. One was the kitchen window while the other
led to a bedroom that was being utilized as a small sewing
room. While the sewing room was empty, the kitchen was
not. I leapt with grace to this ledge. A Kooky Cat Lady
she may have been, but Mrs. Bigg was not untidy. Against
one wall were dozens of tiny dishes—converted butter
and sour cream containers now serving as cat feeders.
Filled with fresh water and dry food, several cats lined up
to have their breakfast. Anxiously I looked from face to
face, seeking that unmistakable thick, velvety blue-gray fur
that Ruby bore. Spotted and calico, white and black, but

no gray. I tapped lightly on the window with my claw. I caught the eye of a wider-than-tall white cat with brown spots, cleaning his paws and ears in a patch of sunlight. He cocked his head, then jumped up to the window, shouldering open the glass but not the screen.

"Hey, pal. You need a home or something?" he asked in a slight Chicago accent.

"No. I'm looking for someone. Name's Ace. I'm a reporter," I told him.

"I see. I'm Boots. Who you lookin' for then?"

I felt my stomach tighten. "Ruby."

He eyed me curiously, his mouth slightly agape. I couldn't help but notice that he had no boots. "Who did you say?"

"A Russian Blue. Gray coat, green eyes flecked with gold." Who was I? A poet? "I thought her name was Ruby but maybe not. Any cat here by that description?"

"Who did you say you were?" If I wasn't mistaken, there was a shred of irritation in his voice. Other cats were beginning to look, curious and about our conversation. Boots was hiding something, I could feel it.

"Name's Ace," I repeated more loudly. "This is a matter of utmost importance."

"What? To exploit?" spat Boots. "I know you media types."

"I'm not here to cause trouble. This cat wants to go home. That's all I want to do, get her home…" I began, but Boots was already shutting the window in my face. A group of other cats gathered in the kitchen, all gazing at me with suspicion.

"Wait! Wait! Boots!" I called desperately as the window gap grew smaller.

"Boots," another voice said. "Wait."

I peered around Boot's massive shoulder.

I caught my breath.

It was Ruby the Russian.

***

Boots glowered at me before plummeting to the floor and stalking off in a huff. Ruby, far more stunning in person than in any of her photographs, sat tall and beautiful in the center of the kitchen floor. Her silver, velvety coat gleamed in the sunshine. Her collar was her signature pink. The Kit-Cat Clock above the stove swung its tail and eyes in opposite directions. Tick, swish, tick, swish.

"Leave us, will you?" she implored of the other cats. They obliged, exiting the kitchen door with whispers and glances back at my precariously perched body. Ruby's dark green, glowing eyes, indeed rich with dots of gold, examined me without prejudice. It felt like she had been waiting for this moment, waiting for me. Seeming to brace herself, she elegantly walked to my window and easily shouldered up the glass.

"Who are you?" she asked. Her clipped tone told me I needed to shoot straight.

"Name's Ace. I'm a reporter, and recreational detective. I was hired a few days ago to find you. By Aero."

Again, I left out the part about being fired.

While her expression remained stoic and unchanging up until this point, she seemed to startle at the mention of Aero. But only momentarily. She recovered quickly.

"Aero?" she echoed nonchalantly.

"Yes, your good friend Aero. He's worried sick about you," I disclosed. Behind Ruby, I could see a gaggle of kittens hunting each other's tails in the living room. A high-backed arm chair sat in front of a tiny television set, where Mrs. Bigg most likely sat each evening. "Ruby, what's going on? How did you get here? We've been all over Lakeville, trying to figure out how you were stolen, how you disappeared!"

Ruby looked down, breaking her mind-bending eye contact. She said nothing. I inhaled.

"I can help you," I told her. She looked up sharply, her jaw tight. Evidently, she was not impressed that I had tracked her down to offer said help. "Ruby, I'm here to get you home."

"This *is* my home."

I hesitated. "No, Ruby, I don't know how this happened to you, but I am going to get you reunited with your family. With Aero. With *Madeline*, Ruby," I pleaded with her stony face. Had I been aiming to speak to her heart, however, I was failing.

"This is my home," she repeated.

For a second, I was at a loss for words. This was not how I pictured finding Ruby the Russian. A bone-crushing hug, yes. A smattering of charm and over-zealous thanks, yes. A pat on the back, yes; but this, no.

"Ruby, I don't understand," I whispered. I could hardly fathom Ruby being held against her will; it made no sense at all. But then again, neither did her attitude.

"And you couldn't. You couldn't possibly understand," her voice cracked. I realized she was near tears. She slammed the window shut, sending me into an acrobatic jump. Ruby leapt from the window and ran from the room.

I stared at the shut window, and the shut window stared back.

Ruby was gone.

## 🐾 CHAPTER EIGHTEEN 🐾

I had her, and I lost her.

My tail hung low as I slowly walked back toward *The Daily Reporter*. My mind was a jumble of racing thoughts. What just happened? *How* did this happen? I solved the crime…yet I hadn't. Somehow, I made it all worse.

The enigmatic Ruby the Russian was found, yet still lost. How was I supposed to reconcile this situation? I couldn't get through to her. It was like she had broken, her spirit crushed.

Lost in my thoughts, wandering near the post office dumpster down the street from *The Daily Reporter*, I hardly noticed when I walked into a big, fuzzy wall.

"Aero! What are you doing here?" I exclaimed, picking myself up and brushing off my fur.

"I wanted to apologize, Ace," the giant German Shepherd said, his eyes sincere. "I wasn't nice the last time I saw you."

"Uhhh," I muttered, at a loss for words. And complete sentences, apparently.

"I just miss Ruby so much. I hate to admit it, but it's true. The house isn't the same without her sassy attitude. It's wearing on all of us, Madeline especially," Aero told me, sitting down and staring off into the deep blue sky.

"Ummmm," I attempted to speak. Well, what was I supposed to say? I found your cat, but she hates you all?

"She just sits around all day, chewing antacids and calling neighbors. Trolling the streets, looking for Ruby. It's depressing," the dog went on. I kept my trap shut. It seemed better that way. I've always been a terrible liar. Perhaps that was why I found companionship with a journalist, not a politician.

Aero heaved a great sigh.

"This has been such a difficult situation, for all of us."

That was a gross understatement.

"But something happened yesterday, Ace. Something that gave me hope, and I knew I needed to find you. Ace? Ace? You look weird. Kinda sick. Do you need me to perform the Heimlich Maneuver?"

"Good grief! No!" I exclaimed as Aero stood up, worry spreading across his face. One more sentimental statement out of Aero, and I was going to fold like a lawn chair.

"Aero, you don't have to apologize to me. Look, I'm sorry, but I'm on deadline," I began, using the ultimate reporter excuse as I backed away from him. "Can we discuss this later?"

"Is something the matter, Ace? You seem strange," he repeated, standing and cocking his head to one side as though to hear me better. It was my turn to heave a great sigh.

"There's something I have to tell you," I conceded. My conscience pulsed with guilt.

"I have to tell you something first," Aero insisted, putting his paw up.

"Well, okay," I hedged.

"We received a ransom letter," he said. Noting my bewilderment, Aero went on, "$5,000 in exchange for Ruby's safe return."

I was speechless. I felt as though I had slipped into *The Twilight Zone*. Mrs. Bigg? Blackmailing the McMahons? It couldn't be.

"I don't understand," I mumbled.

"Isn't this what you've been waiting for? You told me all along it would come to this. I'm sorry I stopped believing it was true. Ruby didn't leave of her own accord. I don't know how someone managed to steal her from under my nose, Ace. But they did. Maybe you were right. Maybe Ellin took her and wants money now."

Ellin's thievery didn't make sense anymore. Why would Ellin nab Ruby just to give her to an old lady? She couldn't exchange Ruby for ransom if she didn't have her. "Do you have the ransom letter, Aero?"

"No, Madeline has it. But I heard them talking about it. You should know she hasn't given it to the police. It specifically stated *not* to contact the authorities, or Ruby would be harmed."

*Mrs. Bigg!* I scolded mentally. Maybe she was ill and needed funds. Perhaps her budget had run dry for shortbread cookies, hard candy that stuck together in a clump, and 75+ women's multivitamins. What other explanation could there be?

"What kind of time limit are we talking?" I asked.

"Tonight. The McMahons are supposed to leave unmarked bills under the mailbox downtown by midnight," Aero reported.

Here? Downtown? Wasn't that risky with so many eyes? Then I realized a quiet business district indeed had fewer eyes than a residential area. There were only a few apartments above the stores, and by midnight those apartments would be filled with nothing but sleeping people, as good as dead to the world. Friday nights were not wild in Lakeville, Wisconsin. Aero went on, "If the exchange goes well, we can expect Ruby in a carrier at our mailbox later tonight."

What was with all the *mailboxes*? I pondered, my mind reeling, trying to process all of the information. Trying to fit together this mismatched puzzle.

"Did you smell this letter?" I asked.

"No. I tried, but Mr. McMahon locked it in his safe. I only heard them discussing it."

"Darn," I cursed.

"Why?"

"You may have picked up a scent, the scent of the thief," I explained. The true thief. There was no way it was the elderly and frail letter-writing Mrs. Bigg. It wasn't Ellin. So who was it?

"Right. I wish I had, Ace. You're a much better spy than I am," he said, shaking his great head.

Something else was going on here. There was some tiny bit amiss that was just out my reach. If only I could think of what it was…it was maddening.

"What are we going to do? What if the attacker doesn't bring Ruby home, Ace?"

Minutes ticked by. I felt like the Kit-Cat clock back at Mrs. Biggs, looking, thinking, looking, thinking. Was this ransom note just some lowlife taking advantage of a grieving family? Did it actually relate in any way to Ruby's disappearance?

I was about to come clean about Ruby's actual whereabouts and ditch the entire ransom charade when a postal worker exited the back of his building, carrying a large cardboard box. It looked as though it was sealed, but he carefully opened it, pulled out a fistful of tissue paper and emptied it into the dumpster. As I watched him brush off his hands and walk away towards a mail vehicle, something hit me with the force of a bird flying headlong into a plate glass patio door.

Mr. X.

"Aero!" I shouted.

"What!" he shouted back.

"Stop the presses!"

"*What?!*" he shouted again.

"What was the mailman delivering that day? The day Ruby disappeared?"

Aero, confused, hesitated. "Huh?"

"You said that the mailman had a package. Remember?"

My heart pounded. Could it be?

"Well, yes. But he was actually *leaving* with a package. I guess I figured it was for another house," Aero's brow furrowed in concentration.

"You're sure? Would your family be sending a package, Aero?"

"No. Mrs. McMahon always goes, well, here. The post office. Sometimes I ride along. Our post delivery man isn't friendly and she hates to bother him. It's one of the many reasons I antagonize him. That, and, of course, sheer principle of the dog-versus-mailman tradition that's been passed down through generations and generations of canines," Aero said proudly. He tilted his head to the side and added, "Why?"

I was certain. I was not certain how I was certain,

but I was certain I was certain.

"Ruby was in the package."

He stared at me as though I'd suffered a serious, albeit unavoidable and tragic brain injury. "I...I...don't think so..."he stammered.

"Listen, Aero. I know it sounds crazy," I spouted off. "Ruby was in that box. The mailman is blackmailing you."

Aero looked unconvinced.

"You told me the mailman delivers stuff to Ruby. Trophies. Food samples. *He knows Ruby.*"

"So?"

"We have no witnesses who saw Ruby leave. No Ruby-scented trail leaving the property, you checked it yourself multiple times. No, Ruby was taken. She wouldn't go willingly. She was nabbed by someone she knew, but it wasn't Ellin. You mentioned you were distracted the day Ruby went missing. The mailman was early that day, he distracted you! It's the same tactic I used the other night to break a cat out of the pound—"

"That was *you*?!"

"—the mailman distracted you, and took Ruby! He's the only concrete suspect within the timeframe of the cat-napping who *left the house*!"

"That's a crummy distraction," Aero muttered.

"But effective," I asserted. "You're a smart dog, Aero. Faster and more ferocious than any dog on his route, I bet. He knew you wouldn't fall for a mystery steak dropped over the fence or a tennis ball tossed down the driveway if he wanted to steal a valuable cat. He used the element of surprise!"

The question was how Ruby ended up at Mrs. Bigg's house. My ever-observant journalistic mind told me Mrs. Bigg was not Mr. X. She hadn't stolen Ruby. So

how—the second favorite question of reporters everywhere—had she ended up there? I didn't know. It didn't
matter. Not yet.

"Which car does your mailman use, Aero?" I
asked.

Still looking befuddled and doubtful, Aero considered. "It looks like that tan Oldsmobile over there, the one
with the 'I Brake for Turtles' and 'Lake Tahoe Makes Me
Smile' bumper stickers. Only, he parks and walks throughout our neighborhood. Ace, if Ruby were in that box, she
would have put up an awful fight, don't you think? How
could he have smuggled her away and into that car?"

"You were distracted, and when you noticed Ruby
was missing, you were all out of sorts. Stronger cats than
Ruby have been smuggled against their will," I noted,
thinking of Sloan's recent unpleasant trip to the vet and
groomer. "Look, your blackmailing mailman is leaving on
his route soon, I'm sure of it. I want you to trail his car
today. Make note of the neighborhoods he visits besides
your own. Find out his name. Meet me at the newspaper
back door at 9 p.m. tonight, and we'll finish this."

Aero raised his ears in disbelief. "What about
Ruby? The ransom? We're cutting it too close! This doesn't
make any sense at all!"

"Don't worry," I assured Aero, "I know exactly
how to get Ruby back. I have a plan."
***

With Aero still in the dark but dutifully trailing the
shifty mailman, I darted over to Sloan's house. The hourglass was quickly running low, and with all of the new
information, I needed to rally my troops.

"So that's the plan," I breathed heavily to my best
friend after telling him the entire story, including Ruby's
bizarre apprehension to return home.

"Plan? You call that a *plan*?!" Sloan cried. "That's not a *plan!* Wake up and smell the newsprint!"

"That's a good line. I should have used that."

"You're outrageous!" Sloan countered, tossing his paws in the air.

"Now that's a compliment. Come now, Sloan, with enough ambitious spirit…"

"Are you out of your *mind?* This will never work, Ace!"

"You've said that before."

"I'll say it again. *It will not work!*"

We stared at each other.

"All right. Now that the outburst is out of the way, will you help me tonight?" I asked calmly.

"Of course."

***

A few hours later in the empty building of *The Daily Reporter*, I paced the floor back and forth. Lately, I've been wearing down the carpet.

It was just past the dinner hour. Darkness was falling fast. Aero was not wrong when he said this did not make sense. He was, in fact, absolutely correct. Had I been writing this up into an article, it would be barely credible enough to print in *The Branford Examiner*. But I was steadfast that my hunch was right. The mailman, for whatever reason, had cat-napped Ruby. Ruby got away safely, finding refuge at Mrs. Bigg's animal rescue emporium. The mailman, not wanting to completely forego his criminal tryst, now asked for ransom and was lying about the safe return of the Russian Blue. What can I say, the man was obviously a crook. What was one more lie going to do to the guy?

It was time to call on Rogue and Co. for the evening's caped crusader events. What was the point of meeting a felon if you couldn't use his lawless skills? So I sent Sloan to the wrong side of the tracks to persuade Rogue and at least a companion or two to join us tonight while I worked on the final details of my masterminded plan of action. Meanwhile, I had one other obnoxious, border-line-criminal "friend" to call upon.

Boris the Rat.

To know him was to loathe him. Such was the trouble with a guy who insisted upon being called not just a name, but an entire title. I swore after this past summer that the next time I talked to Boris would only be to yell at him. But his skills were undeniable, his resources bottom-less. We would need our ratty friend tonight.

Last summer during my first stab at undercover detective work, I was caught, stuffed into a cage, and left for the night before the pound could have me. It was Boris who found me, and Boris who freed me—after a long, lengthy, and painful proclamation that I would not eat him. He also skillfully helped us in taking down the mur-derer. The guy was crafty.

Boris the Rat lived in the basement of a restau-rant just past the downtown district that overlooked a slow-moving portion of the river. He and his wife, Regi-na, recently raised a litter and were now enjoying their post-parenthood freedom. They were both far too sly to get caught by the restaurant staff, who, for some time, tried tirelessly to catch the rat that ate their Raisin Bran. They gave up. You would too if you knew Boris the Rat.

I went looking for Boris at the restaurant. With my claw, I scratched on the glass of a sublevel window. I waited. And waited. Above me, I heard the drone of din-ner conversation, muffled by the floorboards. Florescent lighting cast an unnatural glow over the dead and dying grass where I sat, quickly losing my patience.

"WHAT?!" A gray, furry body with yellow, pointy teeth and long, sticky whiskers sprung up onto the ledge and screwed his face up into mine. With his angry expression and dirty fur, he looked like a quarter when a dollar isn't enough. Only a pane of glass separated us.

"What's your problem, Boris?"

"Boris *the Rat!*" he scolded me, clearly offended.

"Right, Boris *the Rat,*" I corrected myself. "Open this window."

He glowered. I sighed, taking in the sight that was Boris the Rat. His lower half was much rounder than his upper half. Long claws protruded from each of his front paws, which he clenched and unclenched together. His body heaved with each inhale and exhale. Behind him, his long, wormlike tail swished back and forth as his beady eyes bore into me.

"You're looking well," I forced myself to say. A cat backed into a corner will tell you many flattering things.

"Are you here to eat me?" he implored.

"Are we still not over this?" I sighed. He was acting as though I were wearing a bib and sharpening my fork and knife. On the contrary, I have no taste for eating rodents of any kind, most certainly not rats. "Eating, my good friend, is not on the menu tonight."

"Well, then, Ace the Cat, what do you want from me now?" he asked hotly, but I could see he was pleased with my impromptu arrival. His ego was as big as the moon. Boris obliged in letting me squeeze uncomfortably through his basement window. Regina was nowhere in sight. Inside, boxes upon boxes were stacked in every available space. It was cold and dusty. I sneezed.

"So, how's Regina? And the kids? Did they move on to find other businesses to terrorize like their father?"

Boris made a face. "What do you *want*, Ace the

Cat?" he spat, his breath stinking of stale milk.

"All right. I don't like tedious small talk myself," I conceded. "Here it is: I need your help. Tonight."

"Wrong-O, cat!" he laughed, plummeting gracelessly to the floor.

"Aw, really, Boris? I thought we were past all this? We agreed to be friends. Didn't I help you last month get that box of Raisin Bran from the dumpster at the Quick Mart?"

"Boris *the Rat*!" he hissed. "Do you not see that I am busy?" He showed me a metal paper towel dispenser that he presumably dismantled from a lavatory wall. "I am rendering this useless."

"So, you've moved out of the kitchen and are now wrecking havoc throughout the *entire* restaurant?" I asked.

Boris nodded gleefully, his lips curling into a snarl that I can only assume was meant to be a smile. His bulging belly oozed over onto his back feet.

"You don't eat wiring, do you?" I groaned. "You'll burn the joint down. Or get electrocuted."

"I am not that stupid," he threw his words at me, going back to his less-than-handy handiwork. I tried to steer the conversation back on topic. There was nothing Boris enjoyed more than talking about himself.

"Boris the Rat, I call on your skills again," I declared. I tried to see the world through Boris-colored glasses. "As you've pointed out, I am a mere cat. The finery of your anarchic ways against useless humans impresses me, as always. I ask you to help me tonight."

I was right. His attention was piqued.

"You mean to go outside the law again? To take down another human crook?" He put his chin in one filthy paw, thinking.

"I do."

Boris hesitated for an unusually long time, looking into my eyes. I shifted uncomfortably.

"You lie like a rug," he said huskily, pointing an accusing toe at me. I raised my eyebrows. Shoving aside his project, Boris grabbed a nearby fistful of stolen Raisin Bran and munched with reckless abandon, his mouth open and crumbs falling everywhere. "I suppose other *felines* are helping you tonight?" he mumbled over the mouthful of fiber.

I foolishly said there were.

"Cats. Kill. Rats." Boris said definitively, tossing aside a raisin that didn't meet his standards as he launched into his usual monologue. " I will not be had by some ridiculous cat. I will not let any more rat lives be lost to useless, out of control, wild animals like you. I will not die like a rat in a trap."

We've been through this before. *Many* times before.

"Not these cats."

Boris the Rat laughed absurdly, glaring at me over his hairy shoulder. "Why should that be true?"

"My friends didn't eat you last time, did they? They won't this time. You have my word."

"The word of a cat? Ha!"

"Come on, Boris the Rat," I coaxed, now ready to take out my secret weapon. "You're smart."

"I *am* quiet intelligent," he bragged. I cut him off, hoping I wouldn't have to start calling him The *Great* Boris the Rat.

"I've got a box of Marshmallow Munchies with your name on it," I offered.

That finally did the trick, even Boris the Rat couldn't get his dirty little paws on the sugary cereal. I only could because Mary, Sloan's companion, had a sweet tooth for the dental-decaying breakfast treat. I watched

Boris' eyes light up.

"Why did not you say so?" he said in a sickening-
ly nice voice, his cereal forgotten with dreams of sugar
marshmallow hunks in his head. Boris puffed out his ratty
chest. "I suppose I can trust you, even though you are a
*cat.*"

"You trust me? Truly? That means so little."

Boris ignored me. "Indeed, I will help you tonight.
Tell me where to find you."

I told him.

"So, partners again?" I asked with a grimace I tried
desperately to hide, offering an outstretched paw.

"Partners," he agreed, presenting me his own paw
and dirty, protruding claws.

\*\*\*

Free from Boris the Rat and all his perilous antics,
I ran back to the office as the veil of night set in. A low
bark at the back mail slot sent me dashing to see who had
arrived. Was Aero early? He wasn't; the canine in question
was Farfel.

"Ace. I've heard rumblings about the missing Russian. Have you found her yet?" he asked.

That would fall under the headline of "NOT YET
BUT HOPEFULLY DARN SOON."

Instead, I quickly told Farfel everything was underway and that I was still on the story. Truth be told, I sort
of wanted the Saint Bernard to leave. The fewer animals
involved, the better. One shifty set of vermin and a few
alley cats was enough. The clock was steadfastly heading
towards Aero's return at 9 p.m.. Sloan was supposed to
return at any moment, hopefully with Rogue in tow. Un-
trusting Boris would follow within the hour. Anxiety filled
me.

"Head on home, buddy. I'll be by tomorrow," I told

Fafel, trying to shove him off.

"Is there anything I can do to help?" he queried.

"I appreciate the offer, Farfel, but I think I've got it under control. You can go on home."

He looked at me, his already folded Saint Bernard face scrunching up as he scrutinized me.

"I saw that German Shepherd moving through here a few times last week, Ace. Are you telling me you have more than one dog to lend you a paw with this rollicking plan of yours?"

"No, I don't. But..."

"I'll stay then."

"What makes you so sure this is going down tonight?" I asked incredulously.

"I can see it all over your face. You should work on that if you're going to become a feline Dick Tracy," he remarked.

"I don't like the color yellow," I muttered.

At that moment, Rogue's massive form came slinking out of the shadows, Kit Kat and Minx beside him. Minx was scowling. I expected nothing less. Behind them marched Sloan, obviously pleased with himself for convincing the underground cats to join tonight's faction.

"Rogue, glad you could make it. Meet Farfel," I said with a smile. "Farfel, this is Rogue, Minx, and Kit Kat. You already know Sloan, of course."

After awkward introductions, Rogue approached and shuffled me off to the side of the crowd.

"Thanks for coming tonight, Rogue," I said, hoping Rogue was ready to go rogue. Well, more rogue than usual, that is.

"Sure, sure," he reiterated, lowering his voice. "I was actually a bit amped to come along, what with everything I heard about this past summer. But tell me, what kinda human crook are we talkin' about this time? Is it The Moustache?"

"No. Your facts were right, Rogue, but The Moustache wasn't holding Ruby. The man behind the crime appears to be a simple mailman," I explained. "We're taking him down tonight and bringing Ruby home."

"Wait, wait," he exclaimed, holding up paw. "You tellin' me a mailman is holdin' this hot cat?"

"Not exactly," I answered, "but he's behind the masquerade. He must be stopped, he could become the next Moustache. You guys are going to wait here and keep an eye out in case he's early, Aero and I have to finish a little business. Then, just before midnight, we'll get into position. I've got some tuna here to keep everyone happy while you all wait. I have another cat bringing cream and cake."

Rogue eyed me curiously and nodded. "You just like to keep the action rollin' right along, don't ya?" he observed.

I shrugged.

"What's in it for us?"

"I'll owe you a favor," I said.

Rogue rubbed his chin and nodded. "So what you're tellin' me is that we're going to bust a full grown man?"

"That's what I'm telling you."

He examined me under his heavily-lidded eyes and nodded. "Okay, alright. You want me to cough up hairballs? I'll cough up hairballs. We're all in. I hope you're as rough as you act. I even called in Frisky; you remember Frisky?"

I nodded. We shook paws and turned away from each other. At that moment, each of the cats cowered slightly, then raised the hair along their backs. An imposing and impressive figure joined the scene.

"Ease up," I said. "This is my friend Aero."

The giant German Shepherd, shoulders held back and head high, came to my side and nudged me.

"Let's do this," he urged quietly.

With a glance at Sloan, Aero and I were off into the night.

# 🐾 CHAPTER NINETEEN 🐾

Out of earshot of the others, I asked Aero, "What did the mailman do today? Is he the same guy on your route?"

"One in the same. How did you know?"

"A hunch," I admitted. "Did he do anything out of the ordinary?"

"No, though he did seem a little jumpy. Dropped a lot of packages and letters, snapped at an old lady once, tried to pay for a sub sandwich with a roll of stamps. I stayed out of sight, though he was too preoccupied to realize I was there anyway," Aero told me.

"What's his name, Aero?"

"Leonard. Frank Leonard."

I wondered absentmindedly if he had a rap sheet. I didn't have time to Internet stalk him.

"Ace, I still don't understand what's going to happen tonight."

Neither did I, but I'd talked that problem over with myself, and as it turned out, I didn't mind. My utter unease would have to take a backset. I figured it was best to only let myself in on that secret.

"I have to tell you something," I confessed. "We're on our way to a house where a kindly little old lady lives with a whole lot of cats. Ruby is there."

Despite the shock spreading across Aero's face, I quickly went on, "I found her earlier today. She didn't want to leave with me. It's time to play the right card— you. Ruby may not listen to me, but she will to you."

"Wait, wait, wait," Aero interjected, holding up a paw in protest. "Are you telling me that I trailed a mail-man today who doesn't even *have* Ruby?"

"I believe he had Ruby at one point," I said. "From what you tell me, Ruby is a sassy, independent feline. I know you were worried about her, being a housecat and all, but I think she managed to get away from him and found a safe haven here."

"But why didn't she come home?" Aero exclaimed.

"I can't answer that. Ruby will have to. Regard-less, you and I are going to ask Ruby to leave with us, then we're going to alert the police to this blackmailing mailman's less-than-legal activities when he tries to collect the ransom money tonight," I explained. "Ruby, and cats everywhere, won't be safe unless we catch this guy. There's no guarantee he won't try this type of activity again if we don't stop him. Then we'll get those funds back to your companions."

"How?"

"You'll see," I assured him. "It's time to focus on Ruby right now."

Time passed quickly as Aero and I walked the few blocks. The night was clear and cold, with a thousand stars shining above our pointed ears. The full moon was still rising, taking its sweet time. My steadfast demeanor indi-

cated I was fearless and certain, but truthfully I was wildly
uneasy about this entire venture. There were so many
yhings that could go wrong. Too many.

Mrs. Bigg's dark house came into view, an eerie,
flickering blue light emitting from the large front window; the TV was on. I put a paw out to slow down Aero's
determined gait, but he plowed right into me, and we both
ended up tripping over one another.

"All right. This is the house," I panted, brushing
myself off. "We have to proceed with caution."

Aero nodded. His eyes were bright, hopeful.

I described the back porch and the window where
we might be able to catch some feline attention to help
us locate Ruby. Boots would have to respect me with this
kind of backup. My stomach twisted into knots. What
if Ruby didn't come? I told Aero to wait for me while I
peeked into the living room. Approaching the window
flower box, I was careful to not make a noise. Diving
soundlessly into the box, I looked in. Mrs. Bigg was curled
in the armchair, flanked by two tabbies with a soap opera
digest spread open on her lap. Dentures in a cup on the
table and feet propped on an ottoman, she snored deeply.
I jumped down and quickly walked over to Aero, poorly
hidden in the shadow of an oak tree. His ears and eyes
were alert. I motioned for him to follow me. It was time,
not only to find Ruby, but to convince her to leave with us.

Slowly rounding the corner, my heart leapt out of
my chest.

There, velvety gray fur sprinkled with pow-
dered-sugar silver shining in the moonlight, was Ruby. She
sat on the back step, staring at the stars above as though
they held the answers she sought. I exchanged a wide-
eyed look at Aero, his mouth dropped open, large canines
gleaming brightly. Ruby turned slowly and looked at us,

only mild surprise on her face.

The three of locked gazes. After what felt like an eternity, a wide smile that reached all the way to Ruby's green-gold eyes overtook her perfect feline face and she came running right into Aero's chest in a large embrace. He staggered back, then gently wrapped his mammoth paw around her, his face still registering utter astonishment. Rendered speechless, I sat quietly looking on at the reunited pair.

"Aero, I…" Ruby stammered.

"It's okay. You don't have to explain," Aero said quietly.

"But I do, Aero, I do," Ruby began, tears catching in her voice. She looked at me. "I knew. I knew after he showed up today that you'd be along shortly. And the truth is I've wanted to come home. So much. But something held me back."

Aero and I, silent, waited for Ruby to go on.

"I was sick of the shows, sick of the lifestyle. It's so quiet here, so normal. I could go an entire day without preening, days without a bath, without clipping and primping. I could eat without worrying about my waistline. It's been so…freeing."

The giant dog nodded. I think he understood, I think he always had.

"It's not that I didn't miss you all," Ruby continued sincerely, "because I did! So much! All of you, every single minute of every single day. I couldn't bring myself to leave, either. It's been so confusing."

Ruby turned to me, then back to Aero, her eyes pleading. "Surely you understand why I stayed away, just for awhile?"

"But Ruby, how did you leave right under my nose? I've felt like such a failure," Aero said dejectedly.

"Oh, Aero, that's silly. He fooled us, he fooled us all. Most of all, me," Ruby said. "You'll never believe this, not in a million years, but it was the mailman! He cat-napped me!"

Noting our lack of shock Ruby scrunched her flawless face. "What? You knew?"

"Not for long," Aero said. "Ace here put it together."

Giving me a curious expression, Ruby asked, "How?"

"Your mailman, Frank Leonard, may appear to hate dogs, but he actually hates cats!"

I raised an eyebrow. Aero continued to look confused.

"I don't get it," he said, looking at us both. "He hates me. I hate him. It's always been this way, and it always will be. Mailmen hate dogs, dogs hate mailmen."

"I know, I know," Ruby soothed, placing a slightly unkempt paw over his own. "You have to believe me, he actually hates *cats*. Specifically, gray cats. I guess I reminded him of a cat that once bit him as a child. He told me so after he smuggled me out of the house in that cardboard box. He was early that day, he bribed me when I was on my way to the library, saying he had one of my favorite treats inside the package. I was stupid, but I had no reason to believe he would put me in danger. He had, after all, delivered my trophies and ribbons and treats to me before. I guess he was baiting me all along."

"You should never accept treats from a stranger," Aero said.

"Then what happened?" I urged. The story was finally coming together.

"Well, he hustled back to his car—it was so hot in that box, and it was lined so no one would hear me—and finished his route while I was trapped inside. I was so scared," Ruby recalled. "It was hard to breathe. I don't know how much time passed, but when he came back to the car, I was ready for him. See, I used my teeth to cut the padding and tape holding the box shut on the bottom. It was hard, but I didn't get out, not just yet. By then, I was mad."

I marveled at her bravery. What a tail. I mean, what a tale.

"As he drove, he went on and on about how animals like us, specifically cats, did not deserve all those rewards. He said cats were vile creatures and rewarding them was disgusting," Ruby went on. "He said he'd finally thought of the ultimate commodity to steal: a show cat."

"That's terrible," I said.

"Awful. He said that stuff?" Aero mimicked.

"Don't ask me why. Mailmen are known for going postal, aren't they?" Ruby suggested, shrugging.

"Then what?" I asked.

"He came to a stop, and I knew it was time. I could see just a bit out of the opening of the box. I was ready for him," Ruby paused to smile proudly. "When he opened the car door to get my box, I leapt out, hissing and spitting, swatting like mad."

Ruby started laughing, a light, clear sound.

"The look on his face!" she giggled. "You would have thought I was a ninja! It was so satisfying! His eyes got real big, and he stumbled over his own big feet and fell. I think he was still scared of cats, to tell you the truth. Then I took off as fast as I could. I ran and ran and ran, not even aware of where I was going. I avoided the main streets and kept hidden as much as I could. It didn't take much to lose him. I was frightened, yet exhilarated. It was the first time I'd done something on my own. I wandered around a neighborhood for a few hours, smelling the flowers, eating the grass, and talking with a few animals. They told me about this place, Mrs. Bigg's."

We all turned and looked at the tiny house, where inside the sweet old woman slept with her houseful of felines.

"So I came," she said. "I was hungry, after all, and not an outside cat. Nice as it was outdoors, I was ready for some down time. I figured I'd fill up, get some sleep, and try to find home the next day."

The Russian Blue lowered her head.

"Only, I didn't," she confessed. "Mrs. Bigg was so nice, as were all the other cats. They all had fascinating stories and personalities. I missed home, and all of you, so much. I told myself I'd leave the next day, but the days kept going by. I didn't miss the show cat life, you know?"

Aero nodded again, his expression understanding.

"I'm sorry, Aero. That I left you worried and alone. I didn't mean any harm, and I apologize deeply," Ruby said with emotion. She turned to me. "Ace, I am sorry I was rude to you today. That isn't like me. It was just such a shock. I had no idea that everyone missed me as much as I missed them."

"Of course we did, Ruby!" Aero cried. "You're a lot more than just a show cat to all of us! Madeline is putting up posters all across the state and online, running stories in Ace's newspaper pleading for your safe return. They're willing to pay ransom! Everyone is in pieces."

"I don't know…" Ruby mumbled, biting her lip.

"Please. Just come home. I promise it will get better. I can take you outside, on adventures where you would be safe. You don't have to do those stupid shows."

Ruby looked doubtful.

"How?" she asked quietly. "I don't have the nerve

to throw a show."

"We'll figure it out. Together," Aero promised. "We'll dye your fur if we have to. Madeline and Horace will understand."

Still biting her lower lip, Ruby pondered. Then she smiled.

"Okay, I trust you," she said. "Let's go home."

Aero's face broke into a grin and hugged his cat friend again.

"You smell like a real dog, Aero," Ruby's muffled voice came out through his fur.

The canine grinned even wider, obviously pleased that everything was going to be back to normal. Only, just a little different. For the better.

"Here I thought Ellin may have cat-napped you," I confessed. "I visited your three cousins."

"Ellin? Oh, goodness. No, she wouldn't do that. She's unpleasant, but not cruel-hearted," Ruby declared.

"She seemed a bit dodgy, and didn't have an alibi for the time you disappeared," I explained.

"Uno, Dos, and Tres don't know this, but Ellin is sick," Ruby confided. I raised my eyebrows. I could see this was news to Aero as well. "I'm not supposed to know, but I overheard Ellin and Madeline talking a few times over the last few weeks. Ellin has Lyme Disease. It wasn't diagnosed right away, so unfortunately it can be a long and serious sickness."

Boy, did I feel guilty. Stalking and harassing a *sick* woman.

"Gosh, I'm sorry Ruby," I said. "I had no idea. No wonder she looked so peaked and miserable all the time." I smacked a paw to my forehead. "No wonder her hours were long and varied."

"Yes. She'll be okay, after a lot of rest—which she

isn't good at doing—and antibiotics and doctor visits. It's a long and difficult road from what I understand," Ruby said. "I don't think she wanted to worry her cats with her troubles. She should turn to them. She'd feel better if she did."

"I think you're right," I said. I turned to Aero, "We should go."

We all looked longingly at Mrs. Bigg's house one last time, then headed off down the block. Just two cats and a dog out for a late night stroll.

"Oh. Ruby? We have just one more stop before home," I said. "You're going to get a second swat at the mailman who wronged you."

\*\*\*

What was it with crooks and midnight? Something about the witching hour just seemed to trigger all their wicked deeds. Maybe it was a top-rated tip in the *Beginner's Guide to Being a Conniving Thief* manual.

It was 11:30 p.m., the moon now high in the night sky, and the gathering of animals behind *The Daily Reporter* was impressive. As we arrived, my eyes surveyed the lot. Frisky and Farfel sat together discussing about rawhide and real bones, Rogue and Minx lounged with Sloan, sipping steaming milk, and Kit Kat chatted up Lily. I saw Sloan's eyes grow two sizes when he spotted Ruby, glimmering beautifully even under the harsh street lights. He sat up straight, as did Rogue.

"Well, well," droned Rogue, "This must be Miss Ruby the Russian."

"In the fur," she said silkily, shaking paws with Rogue and Sloan, then introducing herself to the rest of the animals. Sloan approached me, still looking at his recently-Ruby-touched paw in awe.

"She's really something, isn't she?"

"Keep the drool in your mouth, Sloan," I said good-naturedly. "We still have work to do tonight."

"Good work, sleuth," Rogue said to me. "You found the missin' cat. Now it's time to make the villain pay. This is *my* area of expertise."

"That's right," I answered.

"Psst. PSSSSSST. Ace the Cat! Over here!"

I looked up. Under the dumpster, crouched in the shadows was a familiar, ratty face.

Boris the Rat.

"Boris. There you are."

"Boris *the Rat*! Come hither at once," he ordered.

Why I listened to him, I couldn't exactly tell you. I guided him just across the back alley. Boris scampered and scurried like a fugitive. I wasn't exactly thrilled about being in the company of a rat, and I'm sure he didn't like being side by side with a cat, but I saw no need to be obnoxious about it.

"I am here," he said in obvious need of great admiration.

"The gratitude parade got stuck in traffic."

Boris ignored me.

"I told you, your clan hates rats," Boris the Rat said smugly under the safety of a car. His fur was heavy and matted, like the material of an antique sofa. "No one will talk to me."

A rat with humility. Who knew?

"Did you introduce yourself?" I asked, though it occurred to me that his personality paired with Minx's would be about as smooth as two freight trains colliding.

Boris shrugged, then said, "I do not like being so close to you." I backed up a few paces. Getting along with this guy was like herding cats.

"Did you bring the industrial strength zip ties?" I

asked Boris, changing the subject. Zip ties, and Boris' ability to use them, were crucial to tonight's plan. It was what made this—being nice to *Boris*—worth all the trouble. He paused and picked a stray blade of grass, gnawing on it with his sharp, yellow teeth. He nodded.

"And you're ready to do as I asked in exchange for the cereal?"

"Why must you ask so many questions?" Boris the Rat snapped.

"This just in: I. Am. A. Reporter," I said, losing patience.

Boris threw his short little arms in the air and tossed his grass aside. "Fine! Let us get on with this!"

"My sentiments exactly."

Walking back, I jumped on top of the dumpster. It was time for me to boost morale. Boris awkwardly joined me, crossing his stubby arms in defiance. I surveyed the crowd, pleased. There was just one important player missing tonight, but she wasn't scheduled to be here. We'd already discussed her role, at a loud volume, earlier that day.

"Hey everyone," I called, my voice raising an octave or two. I preferred to report, not vocalize, to the masses. Everyone grew quiet and looked at me. "Boris and I…"

"Boris *the Rat*," my accomplice hissed under his breath.

"Boris *the Rat* and I would like to say thanks to you all for coming," I proclaimed as I surveyed our crew. I never thought I'd see the day where two dogs, a group of cats, and a couple of vermin would join forces. "Your support tonight is highly valued. You are all doing a brave and honorable deed. We must be careful, though. We all know the plan, and it is important that we stick to it.

Remember, if you are in trouble, get out. If someone else needs your help, prioritize and lend a paw," I took a deep breath. "What we are doing tonight could save innocent lives. What's right is right, and this guy is wrong. So…let's bring him to justice," I finished lamely. Boris shot me an eye roll.

Everyone cheered, slapping paws and nodding. Ruby's green eyes sparkled. Kit Kat sharpened his one fang on a rock. Rogue looked ready to fight, rubbing his massive paws together and sneering appreciatively. Minx glared at Boris, Boris glaring back.

"Let's get into place," Rogue proclaimed.

## 🐾 CHAPTER TWENTY 🐾

In books, they always have a plan. A great plan, with lots of fully-loaded guns, Chuck Norris-style kicks and punches, and something that involves a live trap cobbled together with nothing but the hero's bubble gum and wristwatch.

We didn't have any of that.

One by one, we stealthily headed to the midsection of downtown where the mailbox sat by the curb. A savage howl of wind tore up the street. I ruffled my fur against it and caught my reflection in a darkened but reflective storefront. Black fur, slanted green eyes, determined stance. *I'm a baaaaaad cat*, I told myself.

The group looked at me for further direction. A nearby bench and well-placed trash can provided some cover while other felines would hide in the shadows of entryways. I instructed Minx and Boris to crawl up under the eaves of two separate businesses. I wanted their inflated egos interacting as little as possible.

"Ruby," I said, turning to her a few paces behind

me. "If you want to stay out of the fray, I think that would be best, after all you've been through—"

She stopped me before I could go on.

"No, I do. I most certainly do want in the fray," she assured me, "or at least near it." I smiled and turned to her canine companion, standing close by.

"Aero? Is the money under the mailbox?"

"Yes, I just checked," he answered "The McMahons must have just been here."

"All right, good," I replied. Then louder, I said, "This is it everyone; remember your cues. Off you go to location. Ruby, stay with Aero."

Due to their larger size, Aero and Farfel had to hide the furthest away, down the nearest side street, just out of sight around the corner. Sloan and I took our agreed position in the trash bin nearest to the mailbox. Thankfully, it was emptied by city crew earlier in the evening. All that sat in it was an old copy of *The Branford Examiner*. The sad excuse for a newspaper was in its rightful place, I thought meanly. "ARNOLD TO RUN FOR GOVERNOR IN WISCONSIN," blared an obnoxious headline. I sat directly on top of it.

The familiar scenario of a high-stakes stakeout overtook me. I remembered the past summer when my friends and I stalked the back of a restaurant in hopes of busting a murderous burglar. It was storming that night, and tensions were high. Tonight, I was oddly calm. Perhaps it was because I had so many great animals backing me, or because Ruby was already safely under Aero's watch. Maybe I simply wasn't afraid of a postal worker. Regardless, time passed slowly as my best friend and I waited, silently, inside the trash can on Main Street.

I heard the nearby courthouse clock ring 12 times. Midnight had arrived. We waited on the razor's edge, ready to strike. Slowly the witching hour waned away. Still, we all waited, ready for the pounce. Fifteen minutes went by. Sloan and I shifted uncomfortably and exchanged perplexed glances. Another twenty minutes slowly died.

"Ace?" whispered Sloan.

I looked at him.

"Is he coming?"

I shrugged. A few more minutes passed.

"Maybe we should cut our losses. I don't think we're going to bust the cat-napper this time," Sloan said in a shushed voice. "Let's get Ruby safely home. Her family has worried enough. That's what matters most, isn't it?"

I could hardly argue with that. The clock was ticking away and still, nothing. No one. The stack of money inside an unmarked envelope sat untouched beneath the blue, standard issue mailbox. The mailman turned out to be a chicken.

"Wait here. I'll be right back," I said, leaping from the trash bin. The night was cold and clear, still and without the usual city sounds. I looked up and down the street, trying to catch a moving car, an out-of-place person, or the glint of human eyes. Odd smells. Nothing. There was only silence. Downtown was deserted and lonely. The wind whipped through my fur. Walking away to find Aero, Ruby, and the others, I let my guard down. Just a little, but it was too much.

From behind, I could first sense, then feel, the presence of a man.

My hackles raised, I turned to face whoever had arrived so quickly but was overtaken by a husky figure and nearly crushed by his body weight. His 100-proof breath felt hot on my neck. My lungs flattened, I gasped for another unsuccessful mouthful of air. I struggled furtively against the heavy chest and arms pinning me down, I felt the rough sensation of burlap wrapping around my body and face. My ribs struggled to withstand the pressure, he was stuffing me in a bag. I attempted to hiss and growl and slash with my paws, but it was useless. My whole body was useless. It was like I brought a spork to a knife fight. From inside the scratchy fabric, I faintly heard the barking of dogs. Everything felt fuzzy and dark, it all began to slowly black out.

BARK! RUFF! BARK! GRRRRRRR!

I was 15-years-old and slipping fast.

RUFF! BARK! GRRRRRRR! MEOOOOW!

I wasn't sure if I was going to land on all four feet this time.

MEOOOWWWW! HISSSSS! BARK! BARK! BARK!

Perhaps I should just let go…take a nap…

HISSSSS! RUFF! MEOW! BARK!

It had been such a rough night…

BARK! RUFF! RUFF! RUFF! HISSSSSS!

It was about to get rougher.

\*\*\*

"Ace! DARN IT! Wake up!"

It was Sloan's panicked voice. He shook my body. I heard a painful moan. I vaguely wondered where it was coming from, then realized it was me. I laid limp and lifeless on the sidewalk on top of some type of abrasive cloth. Sloan was still shaking me. What had happened? It was a deadly long time, wasn't it? It seemed as though hours, or maybe days, had passed. Truly it had only been five or six minutes. I raised my head slightly and let my eyes focus. All around me, pandemonium broke loose.

"The dogs pulled you out of the way, Ace," Sloan breathed heavily. "Are you okay? You took a hit! He was hiding downwind in the shadows. I don't know how, and I don't know when!"

I grumbled something about what in the heck was going on. Unable to form words, I coughed and coughed like a luxury car trying to start on cheap gas. Finally, I took in a deep rattling breath of air. The fuzziness in my head faded, I suddenly snapped to attention.

"Whoa, whoa! You aren't getting up, wait here!" Sloan cried, pushing me down as I tried to get to my feet. He took off into the mix.

The scene before me came into full focus. Aero and Farfel and Frisky tore ferociously at the calves and jacket of the blackmailing mailman, who was trying to rage against them all. My friends had the mailman knocked down and pinned, but Frank Leonard was struggling something fierce. Rogue, Lily, and now Sloan were like Halloween cats, backs arched, hissing, paws slashing with claws at full extension. It was a flurry of fur, spit, and claws; they had him completely surrounded. Minx gleefully pulled his hair while Boris the Rat skillfully worked to zip-tie his feet together. Kit Kat was sharpening his claws, courtesy of the mailman's jeans. Ruby stood atop the mailbox, a menacing paw stretched outward as he tried again and again to rise up and grab her, the cat that got away. The Russian Blue bared her teeth, her face filled with anger, her eyes slits of fury. The mailman attempted to recapture his ransom and take down all of us at the same time.

MEEEEOW! HISS! RUFF!

The dogs, cats, weasel, and rat were not having it. Aero snapped at the perpetrator again and again, his massive snout gleaming in fury with a mouthful of sharp, white teeth. Once again, I had been proven wrong and was saved by an overzealous animal's willingness to help— Farfel's enormous body weight and size were definitely keeping the mailman in check, more so as the Saint Bernard came crashing down onto his chest.

"OOOOMMPFFF!" Leonard huffed. *There, how does that feel?*

Frisky was a small but feisty number; his tiny size made it easy for him to zip in and out around the cat-napper, taking bitty nips at his exposed body parts.

"Jeez! Ouch! OWIE! OUCH OUCH OUCH!" he cried, voice thick with pain, as he swatted and swore at his assailants.

The fight was intense and heated, I could stay put no longer. This was my party in the first place.

BARK! HISSSS! MEOWWW! BARK! OUCH! OUCH! BARK! MEOW!

I staggered a bit as I came to all four legs and looked skyward. Right on schedule—and I thanked the heavens she hadn't nodded off to sleep—Birdie was in her window. Her elderly face crinkled into a wide smile as she saw me upright and gave me the paws up. Our plan was underway. It was working. It *had* to work.

RUFF! RUFF! HISS! OWIE OWIE OWIE!

I tried to get into the mix, but it seemed I was barely needed.

"AHHHHHH!" the postal-worker-gone-postal shouted, ultimately overpowered by the animals. Boris successfully restrained the postal worker's feet with the zip ties just as we planned, while Farfel gained further control of him by laying flat on his chest. Aero still barked at an obscene volume directly into his face, and Frisky continued to nip him every few inches.

"Ace!" yelled Ruby. "Get out of the way! Come over here—NOW!"

Ruby jumped from the top of the mailbox to dart underneath, lying on the envelope with her companions' money. I scurried under to join her.

"You're in no condition to fight!" she scolded. "How are you feeling?"

BARK! BARK! RUFF! HISSSS! OUCH!

"I'm fine, Ruby; are you?

RUFF! RUFF! OWIE! MEOW!

"Oh, yes. Though, I'm actually capped," she sighed and showed me a perfect gray-blue paw, ideal apart from the clear plastic caps that kept her from destroying carpet and furniture. "I've tried chewing them off, but it's no use," she shrugged.

"I had no idea," I gasped. "You've made so many daring moves without them!"

She smiled.

OWIE! OWIE! MEOOOOW!

Off in the distance, I heard the wail of a siren. The police were on their way.

"Ruby! The police! We can't let these animals go to the pound. We have to break this up."

BARK! BARK! MEOW! OUCH! OWIE!

"But Mr. Leonard will get away!"

"No, he won't. Boris tied him up. Listen, the police are less than a block from here."

Sure enough, the quiet and shadowy faces of the buildings were awakening with red-and-blue flashing lights. It was just a matter of seconds. The siren screamed again, louder, tearing through the night.

I darted out from my post under the mailbox and hollered, "ROGUE! MINX! FRISKY! KIT KAT! GET OUTTA HERE! *POLICE*!"

Fear registered on Rogue's face. He was not going to the pound again.

"LEAVE! LEAVE NOW!" I urged him. "You've done amazing, thank you, NOW HIGH TAIL IT OUT

OF HERE!"

He did, shortly followed by Frisky; Kit Kat, and Minx. The sirens drew even closer.

"SLOAN, LILY! THAT MEANS YOU, TOO! BORIS THE RAT, GO! FARFEL, BEAT IT!"

Farfel shook his giant head, still holding down the flailing mailman. Aero kept barking, too angry to listen.

"GO, GO, GO—UNLESS YOU WANT TO BE IN RABIES LOCK-UP!" Sloan shouted, backing me up. That got through to them. Farfel hesitantly got up, nudging Aero.

"Let's go," Farfel barked to him. Aero let out one last ear-splitting bark at Leonard and turned to Ruby.

"See you at home?" he asked, voice raspy.

"Of course," she replied. She waved her paw in the air. "Now, GO! It won't do for you to disappear, too!"

Tires screeched, sirens blared, closer every second. Boris the Rat waved to me, grinned, and disappeared down a gutter. Farfel and Aero disappeared down an alley.

"I'll get Lily outta here!" Sloan assured me, pulling her away from the scene. "You've got to leave, too!"

Sirens wailed as cop car rounded the corner, its headlights trained directly on us.

"They know I'm Max's reporter, it's okay. GET OUT!"

Finally, my two friends fled for freedom. I ran to Ruby's side; she looked scared, maybe for the first time. I glanced up at Birdie's window again; there she was, her owner by her side, watching the commotion from their front row seat. The aged cat did just as I asked, or rather, politely screamed. When Leonard showed, I requested that Birdie wake her companion and urge her in every way possible to see the predicted fight on the street, hoping she would call the police. Indeed, tonight, when Leonard attacked me, I was sure her companion showed little hesitation in dialing.

A young cop popped out of the squad car. His lights were still flashing, but the siren was cut. He held his cuffs out at the ready and with a confused look, he examined the scene.

Leonard laid still, his face frozen. His smoldering anger was doused. Ruby and I looked blankly at the officer.

"What in the world…" he began to mutter. Then, he spotted Ruby. Recognition registered in his eyes. "Wait a minute. Is that—?"

Ruby stepped under the streetlight. She lifted her chin, exposing her signature pink collar and silver tag.

"You—you're the missing cat!" he said incredulously.

I nudged the envelope toward him, hundred dollar bills spilling out with a little help from my claws. The cop turned his head to one side, confused.

"I'm Officer Allen with the Lakeville Police Department. Who are you, sir?" he asked Leonard, who most certainly was not going anywhere with the threat of the Saint Bernard and German Shepherd returning, not to mention the zip ties. "Can you tell me what you're doing here?"

Leonard grunted and belched. "I…"

"Are you drunk?" Officer Allen questioned. Leonard shrugged.

Down the street, more sirens screamed. Additional back-up was on its way.

The cop pulled the soon-to-be-former postal worker to his zip-tied feet, the man groaning in defeat. His clothes were tattered from our teeth and claws, his face wet from the slobber of barking dogs.

"Come on, buddy, what's going on here?" Officer Allen asked the mailman again. This time he cackled, a high-pitched drunken cackle. The officer leaned back. "If you don't answer me, I'll have to bring you in for public intoxication."

Another police car arrived. Ruby and I sat single file along the sidewalk like obedient witnesses. From the second squad came the longtime lieutenant, who had frown lines so deep it appeared as though he had not smiled since 1980.

"Officer Allen? What's going on here?" he barked. The phone must have woken him from a warm bed. His eyes burned into the mailman.

"Lieutenant, this man is drunk. He won't answer me. I'm taking him to the station to sober up," he said. "I don't know for sure, but I think he has something to do with the famous missing cat. There she is. She's the spitting image of the posters, right down to the pink collar."

Everyone looked at Ruby. She stood tall and turned her head from side to side, exhibiting the mannerisms she picked up in the cat show circuit. The two cops looked at her in wordless admiration, then snapped back to reality.

"I didn't steal her," Leonard began to say. A thought occurred to him. "I found her! Yeah, yeah, that's it!" His drunken giggle shattered all credibility of that statement.

"What did you say?" the lieutenant interrogated, leaning in his face.

"I want a lawyer," Leonard murmured, hanging his head.

Sounded like the start of a confession to me.

"I wonder if she got loose from him?" Officer Allen observed as he pushed Leonard into the backseat.

"No she didn't! I let her go!" Leonard shouted bla-

---

tantly. Everyone looked at him. "Stupid cat!"

"Repeat that?" hissed the lieutenant.

"THE CAT WAS MINE!" he roared, then burped again.

"TAKE HIM IN!" Lieutenant retorted, not in the mood for his alcohol-induced, cat-napping antics. "Good work, Allen. Let's see if this guy'll talk back at the station. Bag and tag that cash for forensics, will you? I imagine there are some answers there, too. I'll call the McMahons and bring the cat in for identification. How in the world did this man's feet get tied together?" Lieutenant No-Smile questioned. He then focused on Ruby and I. "Here, kitty. Not you. It's that darn, nosy newspaper cat."

Ruby winked at me, then jumped obediently into the backseat of the lieutenant's squad. She knew she'd be home soon, her real home. The lieutenant shut his squad door with Ruby safely inside.

"How, how…how did the newspaper cat find the missing Russian Blue?" Allen said quietly, brow furrowed.

The lieutenant rubbed his forehead, then shook his head as though trying to clear cobwebs. "I'm sure she… this guy probably…well…whatever. You, newspaper cat, go home. Don't you have a story to write?"

Indeed I did.

**CHAPTER TWENTY-ONE**

The next morning came with an appreciation for semi-normal, hectic newspaper days. Max came bustling into the office early, excited to tell me the breaking news— Ruby the Russian's safe arrival back home. I sat perched on his shoulder as he wrote the story, talking to Madeline over the phone. I heard Ruby purring in the background as Max scribbled notes in his usual unreadable-to-anyone-but-him fashion.

Next, Max had a brief but informative interview with Officer Allen, who stopped in the newspaper office later that day. He was shy but authoritative, and had no qualms telling us that Mr. Frank Leonard had been arrested and was expected to be brought up on charges of theft and exploitation. He'd have his initial appearance in court later that afternoon. As it turned out, it wouldn't be the first time he appeared before a judge or slept on a cot with bad springs in the clink downtown. A New Jersey native, the postal worker only recently moved here under a stolen identity of a real mailman after narrowly avoiding felony burglary charges.

Apparently when questioned by the unsmiling lieutenant and Officer Allen, the law-breaking—and highly intoxicated—postal worker rambled like a used car salesman, shamelessly confessing to stealing Ruby in exchange for ransom money. He also proclaimed that just plain hates cats. Eventually, he also confessed to several other petty crimes in Wisconsin as well as his checkered past back in Jersey, taking credit for just about everything but the Kennedy assassination and where he had buried Jimmy Hoffa.

He was fired immediately from the Lakeville Post Office.

Our article, though 15 minutes behind deadline, made the front page. Above the fold it read "BLACK-MAILING MAILMAN NAILED IN ACTION, CHARGES PENDING." Tomorrow, we'd work on an article about the crime of identity theft.

"You shouldn't have been downtown last night in all that action, Ace. Allen told me he saw you there," Max scolded after the newspaper was put to bed. His half smile and the glint in his eye told me differently however, especially when he gave me the larger half of his jelly-filled, heavily-iced donut.

I munched away happily, only slightly sore in the ribcage from last night's assault. Max and I perused the email box for the first time since earlier that day. The news, after all, never quits.

"Look at this, Ace. Another press release regarding an arrest," Max said, sitting forward for a better look at the mug shots. "Too bad it missed the print deadline. We'll have to post it online."

I stopped mid-bite. It was none other than The Moustache and his straggly sister who attempted to squash me the other night. His moustache had not lessened in size, nor had her unibrow. Both wore expressions that showed off their cheerful dispositions.

"Kramer 'The Moustache' Carson and his sibling, Jane 'The Eyebrow' Carson were arrested last night in connection to a series of animal thefts. Anonymous sources have implicated the pair as having numerous stolen, high-value animals in their possession. A witness was able to positively identify the duo by a deep scratch on the woman's face and a heavily-bandaged right hand on the man. They will face a multitude of felony charges following a continued investigation."

I smiled.

"I wonder if they knew the mailman?" Max laughed, sinking his teeth into his gooey pastry. Then, mouth full, "I'm just glad they were all caught."

Me too.

The next day, a letter addressed to Max in shaky handwriting appeared on his desk. It was from Mrs. Louise Bigg. She gratefully commended Max for the uplifting feature story on Ruby's happy reunion with her loving owners.

# EPILOGUE

The next morning saw *The Daily Reporter* flying off newsstands. Scandal sells.

Innately satisfied, I joined Sloan and together we sauntered over to Anne's Coffee Cup to join Lily. She was accompanying us on an invitation to Arbor Vitae Lane, where Ruby and Aero had respectfully requested our company. The sun was shining brightly, and for October, it didn't feel too dreadfully cold.

At our approach, Lily smiled and closed the cover on her paperback where a googly-eyed, love-struck woman coyly ogled a long-haired rose gardener.

"You boys," she attempted to reprimand us. "Will you ever learn? That sure was a narrow escape, especially for you, Ace, Mr. Feline Reporter-Detective."

"I may have been done for, if not for all of you," I admitted.

"But you have to admit, we really made the fur fly!" laughed Sloan, patting Lily and I on our backs.

The three of us walked, enjoying the warmth of

the sun. Above the quilting shop, we all paused and waved at Birdie, taking in the glorious fall day from her window perch. I'd sent her a new catnip mouse, something a faithful reader once gave me but would be much better loved by the elderly cat. Birdie waved excitedly, holding up the new mouse for me to see. It was already missing one eye.

She was not my only debt to repay. Last night, Boris the Rat arrived at my back step, demanding his box of sickly sweet cereal.

"Well, Ace the Cat. We did it again. Did you ever think you would be in cahoots with a rat?" Boris asked me. "What a peculiar friendship."

"It's everything I never wanted, and so much less," I grinned. He left with the box of cereal, towing it behind him with a rope. If he noted the absence of a silver platter when I gave it to him, he had not commented.

At the McMahon home, Ruby—not Ruby the Russian, just Ruby—sat on the porch. Aero, wearing a fetching red bandana around his neck, was at the base of the steps keeping a watchful eye over his homestead. Ruby leapt from her spot and barreled over to us, acting just like any other common housecat. She hugged each of us, lingering slightly longer when she got to me. Aero followed, tail wagging.

"Ace, I can't convey my gratitude enough for all you've done," Ruby said. "You were all so brave."

"Hey, pal," Aero said to me. "Thank you for sticking to the story, even when I told you not to."

I nodded sheepishly.

As we all made our way to the back garden, we went over the wild events of the night Frank "The Mailman" Leonard was taken down. It was the kind of conversation you could only have after you've been through such a life-changing event that had turned out so well.

Turned out well, it had.

Ruby was no longer a show cat. The McMahons were overjoyed to have their companion back and wanted to simply enjoy being a family again. Having Ruby in those high-class shows was too much of a risk, they said. It was time to partake in the simple life. Ruby was thrilled, having not even bothered to lick her fur that day, nor her paws. She could just be a simple, lazy housecat now.

"Hey, guys, remember when I cornered you under the kitchen window here?" laughed Aero. "You guys were so scared I thought you were both going to drop dead!"

"Oh. Oh, yeah. That was fun," Sloan said without conviction.

In the backyard, a picnic of sorts was spread out clumsily by Aero and Ruby, with a selection of salmon, tuna, shredded chicken, cheese slices, and whip cream. From around a hedge came the identical smashed faces of Uno, Dos, and Tres.

"Ace!" Uno called to me.

"Uno! Hi, Dos, Tres," I said. They ignored me, heads held high as they approached Sloan. I guess they still found my attitude lacking.

"What a great mystery you guys solved," Uno said. "I'm so delighted you helped bring Ruby home safe and sound."

"I appreciate you saying so, Uno."

Everyone dug into the food, conversing happily. Along came Farfel, carrying a large milk bone for Aero. He hadn't slobbered on it too much.

"Cripes. I just barely got away from Fifi and Fluffi!" he groaned. "Those darn, prying, yapping, bedazzled-sweatered, toy poodles!"

Even that made us all hoot with laughter.

"Ace, aren't Rogue and his crew coming?" Ruby

asked suddenly.

"No. They plan to take a much-needed vacation, what with the animal smugglers behind bars now. I think they were planning to visit the aquarium today and the bird sanctuary tomorrow. I know Minx was hoping to find an all-you-can-keep-down buffet," I explained, having spoken with Rogue after Boris left.

Against the odds, Rogue and I also become tentative friends. "Well-played, pal," Rogue had said to me, a wry half smile on his face as he promised to visit again soon. "Keep in touch. You might be an underground cat after all."

Last, but certainly not least, came Ally and Peter. While this was their first time meeting Ruby, Sloan and I had explained their integral role in our detective endeavors. Ruby welcomed the brother and sister with open paws. Peter dove headfirst into the dish of whipped cream; he emerged as a tiny Santa Claus.

"Ace! So good to see you!" he exclaimed in his usual high and squeaky voice. "I was just writing a story about Henny Penny and her allegation of the sky falling. It was a farce. It was just a pine cone planted by the CIA."

We all smiled, and Peter mimicked us.

"What do you say, big shot reporter?" Ally teased me, rubbing my shoulder with her own. "Had enough of playing in the big leagues?"

"Ah, Ally. You know the news never sleeps," I retorted.

Just then, footsteps at the front of the house sent Aero into a frigid state of anticipation; Farfel was brought to immediate attention as well.

"Excuse us ladies, gentleman," Aero proclaimed properly. "We have a new mailman to scare the shorts off of."

BARK! BARK! BARK! BARK!

With amused silence, I watched them go. Just I was about to dig into a donut when I felt a nudge at my side.

"Psssst…Ace."

It was Uno. She looked nervously over her shoulder. "I think I've got another story for you."

**-END-**

## About the Author

A.M. Bostwick has loved reading and writing since childhood. A University of Wisconsin-Stevens Point graduate, she has worked in journalism for most of her career. An early draft of her young adult novel, "Break the Spell," was finalist in the 2013 Wisconsin Romance Writers of America Fab 5 Contest. Abigail lives in northern Wisconsin with her husband, dog and thrill-seeking cat.